FAIRY CHARM

A charm bracelet opens
a magical world of adventure

**Enter the magical world
of the Fairy Realm!**

Jessie goes to stay with her grandmother
in her rambling old house and discovers an
amazing secret – a magical door in her
grandmother's garden opens into a real
fairy world. In the magical Fairy Realm
Jessie makes friends with unicorns, mermaids,
pixies, elves and lots and lots of fairies!

Jessie's magical new friends leave her a lovely
charm bracelet. And each time she visits the
Realm she is given a brand-new charm!

The **Fairy Charm** series
by Emily Rodda

FAIRY CHARM

A charm bracelet opens
a magical world of adventure

The Charm Bracelet

EMILY RODDA

Catnip
PUBLISHING LTD

CATNIP BOOKS
Published by Catnip Publishing Ltd
Islington Business Centre
3-5 Islington High Street
London N1 9LQ

This edition first published 2006
1 3 5 7 9 10 8 6 4 2

First published in 2000 by the Australian Broadcasting Corporation,
GPO Box 9994 Sydney, NSW 2001

Text copyright © Emily Rodda, 2000

A CIP catalogue record for this book is available
from the British Library

ISBN 10: 1 84647 010 2
ISBN 13: 978-1-84647-010-3

Printed in Poland

www.catnippublishing.co.uk

Contents

The Secret Garden

essie felt better once she was in the secret garden. She sat down right in the centre of its smooth, small square of lawn and looked around.

Yes, here at least nothing at all had changed. This place still made her feel as safe and peaceful as it always had. Clustered around the edges of the lawn, her grandmother's favourite spiky grey rosemary bushes still filled the air with their sweet, tangy smell. Behind them the tall, clipped hedge still rose high on every side. When Jessie was little, she used to think the hedge made this part of her grandmother's garden very special. Its wall of leaves seemed to keep the whole world out.

But, thought Jessie, clasping her hands around her knees, it doesn't keep the world out. Not really. The secret garden's just a place at the bottom of Granny's real garden. It's a place where I can be alone for a while, and pretend things are still the way they were before Granny fell and sprained her wrist. Before Mum started worrying about Granny living alone, and decided she *must*, absolutely must, move out of Blue Moon, her big old house in the mountains, and come to live with us.

She remembered the last time she and her mother, Rosemary, had come to stay with Granny. It had been winter, nearly three months ago. There had been no talk of Granny moving then. Then, things had been very different.

Jessie had always loved winter at Blue Moon. Every evening, as it got dark, they would light a fire in the living room, and then Jessie and her mother would sit cuddled up on the big squashy chairs watching the flames while Granny made dinner.

'No, I don't want help. You sit down and rest, Rosemary,' Granny would say to Mum. 'You work too hard. Let me look after you—just while you're here. I love to do it.' And after a few minutes' protest, Mum would agree, and settle back gratefully, smiling.

Then for a while the only sounds they would hear would be the popping and snapping of the fire, the purring of Granny's big ginger cat, Flynn, crouched on a rug, and Granny's voice as she moved around the kitchen, singing the sweet songs that Jessie remembered from when she was a baby. There was one song that she had always especially loved. *Blue Moon floating, mermaids singing, elves and pixies, tiny horses …* it began. Jessie thought Granny had probably made it up, because it didn't rhyme, and the tune was lilting and strange.

Inside Blue Moon it was warm, cosy and safe. Outside, huge trees stretched bare branches to a cold black sky that blazed with stars, and in the morning a dusting of white frost crackled under your feet when you walked on the grass.

It had always seemed strange and magical to Jessie. At home there were no big trees and no frost. And the city lights seemed to drown the brightness of the stars.

But if winter in the mountains was magical, spring was even better. In spring everything sparkled. The bare trees began to bud with new leaves of palest green, and in their shade bluebells and snowdrops clustered. Bees buzzed around the lilac bushes that bent their sweet, heavy heads beside the house. Butterflies of every colour and size danced among the apple blossom. In spring it was as if Blue Moon was waking up after a long sleep. Everywhere there were new beginnings.

But not this spring, Jessie thought sadly. This spring was more like an ending. She'd been feeling sad ever since her mother had told her about the plan to take Granny home with them at the end of this visit.

'Don't you want Granny to live with us, Jessie?' her mother had finally asked her, as they drove up the winding road that led from the city to the mountains. 'You two have always been so close, especially since your dad died. I thought you'd love the idea.'

Jessie tried to explain. 'It's just that ... I can't really imagine Granny away from Blue Moon,' she said. She turned her head away, pretending to look out the window, but really not wanting her mother to see the tears she could feel prickling in her eyes. 'And ... I'll miss ... coming up here,' she burst out. 'I'll miss the house, and the trees, and the secret garden.'

'Oh, darling, of course you will!' Mum took one hand off the steering wheel to stroke Jessie's long red hair. 'So will I. Blue Moon's my old home, remember. I love it, just like you do. But Jessie, it's been five years since Grandpa died. And you know how worried I've been about Granny living all alone without anyone to look after her.' She smiled. 'My dad might have been the artist in the family, but he was a very practical man all the same. You wouldn't remember, I suppose. But he was sensible, and took no risks. Which is more than you can say for Granny, bless her heart.'

Jessie in fact did remember Grandpa quite well, even though she'd been so young when he died. His name was Robert Belairs. His paintings had been sold all over the world and were in many books. But to Jessie he was just Grandpa, a tall, gentle man with kind blue-grey eyes, a short white beard and a beautiful smile. She remembered how he always let her watch him paint in his upstairs studio at Blue Moon. And she remembered the paintings he worked on there—the soft, misty mountain landscapes, and the fairyland scenes for which he'd become so famous.

It was the fairy pictures that Jessie had

especially loved. Sitting quietly on a stool beside him, she used to watch with wonder as a fantasy world came to life under her grandfather's brush, a mysterious and beautiful world full of golden light. Lots of these paintings hung on the walls of Blue Moon, because every year, on Granny's birthday, Grandpa had painted a special picture just for her. He'd finished the last one just before he died.

Robert Belairs' fairyland was a world of pretty cottages, treehouses and shining castles, and elfin-faced people in wonderful floating clothes. He always called these people 'the Folk'. The most beautiful and royal-looking of the women had long golden-red hair and green eyes like Jessie's own. This had pleased her very much, though she knew that Grandpa wasn't really painting her. He'd always painted his fairy princesses that way. People used to laugh and say that was why he'd fallen in love with her grandmother in the first place. Granny's hair was white now, of course, but when she had first come to Blue Moon to marry Robert Belairs her hair had been as red as Jessie's.

Grandpa's paintings were also full of busy gnomes, dwarfs, pixies and elves, thin little brownies, and tiny flower and rainbow fairies with gossamer wings. There were sometimes miniature horses, too, their manes threaded with ribbons and tiny bells. Jessie had really loved those. She had thought her grandfather was very clever to be able to paint such pictures. Maybe he was a bit magical himself.

And yes, she remembered how carefully he had looked after Granny, too. When Mum and Jessie had visited Blue Moon in those days, it was Granny who cooked the delicious food they ate, who talked and laughed, who suggested all sorts of outings and adventures and never expected anything to go wrong. But it was Grandpa who packed the extra box of matches for the picnic, 'just in case'. It was Grandpa who took the umbrella when they went on a walk, 'just in case'. It was Grandpa who made sure there were spare keys to all the doors, 'just in case'.

Granny used to tease him about it. She'd reach up to pat his cheek, the gold charm bracelet she always wore jingling on her wrist. 'You always expect the worst, Robert. Don't worry so. All will be well,' she'd say. And he'd smile, and touch her hand. 'Better to be safe than sorry, princess,' he'd answer. And quite often he was right.

Jessie could understand why Mum thought Granny couldn't exist safely without him. But she just knew Mum was wrong. Her mind went back to the argument they'd had in the car on the way up to Blue Moon.

'Granny tripped over that stray kitten that came in!' she'd protested. 'That had nothing to do with being alone, Mum. That could happen to anyone, any time. And she only sprained her wrist.'

'But Jessie, it could have been so much worse!' Her mother had frowned. 'If she'd hurt her leg or something she could have lain there in pain for days without being able to call for help.' Her hands had tightened on the steering wheel. 'You have to be sensible about this, Jessie,' she'd said firmly. 'And so does Granny. Both of you have to listen to me for a change. What's needed round here is a bit of common sense!'

Now, sitting in the secret garden, Jessie realised that her mother was really very like Grandpa. She had his kind blue-grey eyes and his strong practical streak. She wasn't like Granny at all. But Jessie was. She knew that quite well. For one thing, she looked like Granny. She was going to be taller, of course: that was obvious, since already they were about the same height. Jessie wore an old grey cloak of Granny's for a dressing gown when she came to stay at Blue Moon, and even when she was in bare feet it didn't trail on the ground.

It was from Granny that Jessie had inherited her red hair, green eyes and pointed chin. She had been named Jessica after Granny, too. But, more important than name or looks, Jessie and her grandmother shared a love of stories, songs and fantasy that made them really enjoy each other's company.

And there was something else. They simply understood each other. Jessie always knew how Granny was feeling about things, and Granny always knew how Jessie was feeling, too. It had been like that ever since Jessie could remember.

Was that why, when Jessie had run into Granny's bedroom after they'd arrived at Blue Moon an hour ago, she had immediately felt so worried and sad? Was that why she hadn't been able to bear staying there, but had had to escape to the secret garden? Was that why …?

Jessie sat perfectly still. Without warning, a thought had whirled into her mind. She began to shiver, her eyes wide and startled, her hands gripping the soft grass. Suddenly she had become terribly sure of something. Granny was in trouble. Real trouble. It wasn't just a matter of a sprained wrist, or sadness, or loneliness. It was something far more dangerous.

She sprang to her feet. She didn't know where the thought had come from. But now it was there, she knew it was true. And she had to do something about it. She didn't know what. But she had to help. She had to!

She began running for the house.

CHAPTER TWO

The Missing Bracelet

At her grandmother's bedroom door Jessie hesitated. Her heart was thumping. She smoothed her tangled hair and tried to calm down. Mum and Nurse Allie would still be with Granny. They'd be alarmed if she burst into the room in a panic.

She felt the soft tap of a paw on her ankle, gasped with fright, and looked down to meet the solemn golden eyes of Flynn, her grandmother's cat. He had been sitting so quietly in the dim hallway that she hadn't noticed him. She crouched to stroke his soft fur.

'Are you keeping guard on Granny's door, Flynn?'

she asked him. 'Won't Nurse Allie let you inside?'

He stared at her, unblinking.

'She would, you know, if only you wouldn't fight with the grey kitten,' Jessie whispered, moving her hand around to scratch him under the chin. 'It wasn't the kitten's fault that Granny fell, you know, Flynn. It was an accident.'

Flynn rumbled in his throat, a noise more like a growl than a purr.

'Don't worry,' Jessie soothed him. 'Granny will be feeling better soon. Nurse Allie's going home now that we're here. Mum's a nurse, too, and Granny will be quite all right with her. So tonight I'll let you into Granny's room. The kitten can stay out, for a change. Everything's going to be all right, Flynn.'

But when she opened the door and slipped into the bedroom, she wasn't so sure. When they'd first arrived, Granny had been sitting in her comfortable chair by the window. Now she was lying in bed, looking pale and ill. Rosemary was sitting beside her, hands clasped on the flowery bedcover, while in the corner of the room Nurse Allie, plump and busy, measured out medicine. The little grey kitten, Flynn's enemy, purred softly on the window seat.

Granny's long white hair, braided into a thick plait, trailed over the pillows. One wrist was heavily bandaged. The bandage was much more obvious now that she was lying down and her arm was out of the sling she'd been wearing earlier.

She smiled faintly at Jessie. 'Where have you been, Jessie?' she asked. Even her voice sounded different. It seemed to have lost its music.

'I've been to the secret garden,' Jessie said, moving over to stand beside the bed.

Granny smiled again. 'Oh, yes,' she murmured. 'The secret garden. You love it, don't you, Jessie?'

'Maybe you could come there with me, tomorrow morning,' Jessie suggested eagerly, taking her hand.

'Well, that might be a little difficult for Granny, dear,' beamed Nurse Allie, bringing the medicine over to the bed. 'But you could sit out on the front verandah for a while, Mrs Belairs, couldn't you? The fresh air would do you the world of good. Cheer you up!'

'We'll see,' said Granny softly. 'I just feel … so tired.' Her eyelids fluttered closed.

Jessie looked despairingly around the room. Why was Granny like this? She saw that Nurse Allie was shaking her head at Mum in disappointment. Cheerful Nurse Allie, with her crisp curls and smart uniform, had tried very hard to make things pleasant for Granny while she waited for Mum and Jessie to come.

She'd used every trick she knew to brighten up the bedroom. She'd brought in vases of spring flowers. She'd opened the curtains to let in the sunshine. She'd let the grey kitten play on the rug. She'd noticed that the dark, mysterious painting on the wall facing the bed, the last painting Grandpa had done before he died, made Granny cry, so she'd taken it away and put a pretty mountain scene in its place.

But nothing had worked. Granny lay quiet and listless in her bed, or sat obediently in her chair, without showing any sign of cheering up or getting well.

Jessie was still for a moment. Then she noticed something. She stared. Why hadn't she noticed this before?

'Granny, where's your bracelet?' she asked. Never before had she seen Granny without her gold bracelet, so thickly hung with charms that it tinkled on her wrist with every movement.

The old woman's eyelids slowly opened. 'Bracelet?' she mumbled. She looked confused, and then there was a flash of memory and panic in her eyes. Her fingers tightened on Jessie's hand. 'It's lost!' she muttered. 'Jessie ... it's gone. They ... must have taken it off while they were fixing my wrist.' She struggled to rise from her pillow. 'Jessie, you must find it for me. You must! I need it!'

'Now, now, don't let's get ourselves into a froth!' crooned Nurse Allie, frowning at Jessie. She pressed Granny gently back on to the pillows. 'Now, we've been through all this, dear. We know the bracelet must be somewhere, don't we? It's quite safe. It's been put away in some drawer or other, that's all.'

'I must have it!' protested Granny, moving her head restlessly.

'You just concentrate on getting better, Mum,' said Rosemary. 'We'll worry about the bracelet later.'

'But time is running out! It's nearly my seventieth birthday!' Granny cried. Then she stopped, and a strange, puzzled expression crossed her face. 'My birthday? Why does that matter?' she whispered.

Nurse Allie stepped forward briskly. 'A little rest is what you need, I think, dear,' she said, shooting a warning look at Rosemary and Jessie. 'All this excitement! Goodness me!'

'Sorry, Nurse,' said Rosemary. She stood up and pushed Jessie a little crossly to the door. Jessie could see there was no point in arguing. Both Mum and Nurse Allie thought she was making Granny upset. She let herself be ushered from the room.

Flynn looked at Jessie and her mother with wide eyes as they closed the door softly behind them, but he made no move to follow them out to the back of the house. He just settled back to his guard duty, still as a statue, in the dim hallway.

'Jessie, you mustn't worry Granny,' Rosemary said sternly as they reached the kitchen. 'Not about the charm bracelet, or the secret garden, or anything. She's not well. She has to have peace and quiet.' She began pulling things out of cupboards, getting ready to start dinner. Then she turned around and tried to smile.

'Look, darling, don't worry too much,' she said. 'It's only natural for Granny to be depressed. Just think about it. Her wrist must be very sore. And it's her birthday the day after tomorrow. It wasn't long after her birthday five years ago that Grandpa died. It makes her sad to think about it.'

'But Mum ...' Jessie looked at her mother's

kind, worried face and thought better of what she'd been about to say. Mum wouldn't understand about the feeling of danger she'd had in the secret garden. And she wouldn't understand why she felt the charm bracelet was so important. After all, Jessie didn't really understand it herself!

All Jessie knew was that Granny was in trouble. And that the charm bracelet she always wore was missing. And that for some reason the bracelet had to be found before Granny's birthday the day after tomorrow. Jessie clenched her fists. She made herself a promise that she would find the bracelet if she had to look behind every cushion and in every drawer in the house to do it! After dinner she'd check Granny's room. Then she'd do the living room and the kitchen. She'd be sure to find it before bedtime.

But bedtime came and still the bracelet had not been found.

Jessie lay cuddled up in bed in the small room that was always hers at Blue Moon and thought hard. Of course there were many more places she could look. But she couldn't see how the bracelet could have got into one of the spare rooms, for example, or the dining room, or the sunroom either.

She closed her eyes. The bed was warm and soft, and the sheets smelled faintly of rosemary. She was very tired. Her thoughts began to drift. In the morning she'd try again. In the morning …

Her eyes flew open again. She could have sworn she'd heard a very faint tinkling sound. It sounded just like the charm bracelet when it jingled on Granny's wrist. And it had come from outside, in the garden. She was sure of it.

She threw back the covers, jumped out of bed and ran to the window. Outside, grass and flowers shone in the moonlight. The trees held their budding branches up to the sky, throwing deep shadows on the lawn. Jessie strained her eyes, but there was nothing more to be seen. Nothing but the grey kitten, slinking through the trees towards the secret garden.

Jessie shivered. She left the window and ran back to bed, jumping in and pulling the covers tightly around her. There was no one out there. She must have imagined the sound. She closed her eyes again and tried not to think about the bracelet. Again the warmth of the bed stole around her. Then, suddenly, she thought of a place she hadn't looked. When Nurse Allie had taken Grandpa's painting off Granny's bedroom wall, she'd put it in his studio for safekeeping. Jessie heard her tell Mum so. Maybe she'd absentmindedly put the bracelet there, too.

The more Jessie thought about it, the more likely it seemed. The studio. First thing in the morning, she'd look there. With a sigh of relief she turned on her side, and in a few moments was asleep.

CHAPTER THREE

The Call

The next morning, before breakfast, Jessie went to Grandpa's studio. She turned the key in the door and let herself in. It was a big, beautiful room painted white. The early morning light streamed through its tall windows.

Jessie sighed. The room reminded her so much of Grandpa. It still smelled of paint, canvas and paper. The stool she had always sat on while she was watching him paint stood in one corner. His paints and brushes, sketchpads and other things lay on the bench as though he was about to come and use them any minute.

She noticed that the picture Nurse Allie had

taken from Granny's room was leaning against a table near the door. She looked at it curiously. It certainly wasn't as pretty as most of the others Grandpa had done, she decided. It was dim and very mysterious-looking, and there were no people, animals or fairies in it. It showed an archway in a wild-looking, dark-green hedge covered with splodges of grey. Through the archway you could dimly see what lay beyond—a pebbly road, a few shadowy bushes and a grey sky in which a pale blue moon floated. A blue moon, thought Jessie. Grandpa must have been thinking about this house when he painted that.

Carefully she tipped the painting forward so she could look at the back. She knew Grandpa often put the names of his paintings there. But this time there was no name. Only a white card, painted with a sprig of rosemary, and some words in Grandpa's firm, looping handwriting: *For my princess on her birthday. Better to be safe than sorry. All my love, always, Robert.* Then there was a date. Almost exactly five years ago.

Holding her breath, Jessie gently let the painting tip back into place again. No wonder it made Granny cry. It mightn't be the prettiest picture Grandpa had painted, but it was his last present to her, and the message showed how much he'd loved her.

Biting her lip, Jessie looked around at the benches and shelves that lined the studio. Everything was neat and clean. Everything was in its place. There was no sign at all of the charm bracelet.

She left the studio and hurried to Granny's room. She found her sitting in her chair by the window, her arm in a white sling. Flynn, purring like rumbling thunder, was lying beside her. The grey kitten was nowhere to be seen. Granny looked up and smiled as Jessie came in and gave her a kiss.

'Your mother was wondering where you were, Jessie,' she said. 'I think she wants you to have breakfast.'

'I've been looking for your bracelet, Granny,' said Jessie eagerly. 'I haven't found it yet, but I just came to tell you that you mustn't worry. I won't give up. I'm going to look everywhere till it's found.'

Her grandmother's smile slowly faded and a puzzled line deepened between her eyebrows. 'Bracelet?' she asked softly. 'What bracelet is that, Jessie?'

Shocked, Jessie stared at her. 'Your charm bracelet!' she burst out. 'You know. The bracelet you always wear. The one that got lost.'

'Oh ...' Granny looked confused and uncertain. She raised her unbandaged hand to her forehead. Her fingers trembled slightly. 'Oh ... I'm sorry, dear. I'm ... getting a bit forgetful, I think. I'm not quite sure ...'

Flynn growled in his throat.

'Breakfast, Mum!' announced Rosemary's cheery voice. She came in bearing a tray of fruit, toast and tea, and put it down on a side table. 'Oh, here you are, Jessie!' she exclaimed. 'I didn't know where you'd got to.'

Jessie looked from Granny to her mother and back again. Her throat felt tight. Only yesterday Granny had been worrying herself sick about the charm bracelet. How could she have forgotten it so soon? She mumbled something, backed out the door and ran for the kitchen.

Jessie searched for the charm bracelet all day, but when night fell she still hadn't found it. And she was the only one who cared. Granny now seemed truly to have forgotten that the bracelet had ever existed. And Mum, busy packing and organising things for the move back to town, was too distracted to think much about it.

'Don't worry yourself too much, Jessie,' she said kindly that evening, as she watched Jessie going through the drawers in the living room yet again. 'The bracelet's slipped down behind something, probably. Or got mixed up with some other stuff in Granny's room. It'll turn up in the end.'

Maybe, thought Jessie. But not soon enough. Tomorrow's Granny's birthday. We're running out of time. She paused, confused by her own thoughts. Running out of time? For what? She closed the drawer in which she'd been searching, and rubbed her forehead with a tired hand. Mum had said not to worry but Jessie couldn't help it. And something else was worrying her far more than the missing bracelet.

She glanced at her mother. She couldn't keep it to herself any longer.

'Granny doesn't remember her bracelet any more!' she whispered. 'When I talk to her about it she doesn't know what I mean!' She bent her head, tears in her eyes.

Rosemary's face softened. 'Oh, Jessie, darling, don't be sad.' She put her arm around Jessie's waist. 'You know that sometimes when people get older they can be forgetful. And Granny hasn't been well. She had a bad shock when she fell. It's quite natural that she's a bit confused now. It's not something to be scared of or anything.'

Jessie nodded and sniffed. 'I know that,' she said. 'But Granny's not very old. She's only sixty-nine. Simone at school's great-grandmother is a hundred and one, and *she* remembers things. And anyway, Mum, whatever else Granny forgot, how could she forget the charm bracelet? She used to tell me every charm on it was a memory of something special. Every charm had a story. The heart, and the fish, and the apple, and the key, and ...'

Her mother patted her shoulder. 'I know,' she soothed. 'I know. It's hard for you to understand. But Granny's been living alone here for too long, Jessie. She's been living in the past. She'll be so much better when she's away from here. Believe me.'

Jessie wasn't so sure. When she crawled into bed that night, her thoughts were racing around in her head so much that she was afraid she would lie awake all night. But she was very tired and it wasn't long before she was lulled to sleep in the warm, cosy bed.

She slept very deeply. The moon climbed higher in the sky and shone through the window, but Jessie slept on. There were sounds in the night but she didn't hear them. The hours slipped by. And then …

Thud! A heavy weight landed on Jessie's feet. She opened her eyes, blinking in the darkness. Her heart pounded. What was happening? She felt something moving on the bedclothes. And then she was staring into the golden gaze of Flynn, and his soft paw was patting her cheek.

She wet her dry lips and sat up. 'What is it?' she whispered. Flynn stared at her, then looked towards the window.

Jessie rubbed her eyes. Was this a dream? No, Flynn was really there, and again he was looking at the window. He jumped from the bed and walked over to it, his tail high. He looked back at her. He wanted her to come with him.

Jessie got out of bed and went to the window just as she had the night before. She looked out. But again there was nothing to be seen. Not even the grey kitten, slinking among the trees. There was nothing …

And then she heard it. The faintest possible sound. A voice. She strained her ears to hear.

'Jessica! Jessica!'

Jessie's mouth fell open in shock. Someone was calling her name! She looked wildly at Flynn. He padded to the bedroom door, looking back at her over his shoulder.

'Flynn, what is it?' hissed Jessie. He went out the door and then came back in again. His golden eyes were fixed on hers. It was obvious that he wanted her to follow.

'Jessica!' The voice was a little clearer now. It sounded urgent, and tired, as though it had been calling for a long time.

Jessie ran to the corner cupboard and pulled out Granny's old grey cloak. It would be chilly in the garden. She threw the cloak around her shoulders and followed Flynn.

He padded to the back door and then stood back while she opened it and slipped outside into the cool night air.

'Aren't you coming with me?' she whispered, looking back at him. But somehow she knew the answer even before he sat down on the doorstep, head up, paws pressed together. He had to wait here. He had to guard Granny. That was his job.

Jessie had to go into the night and answer the strange call alone.

She began to creep through the shadows on the lawn. The voice was clearer now, though it was still faint. And she thought that behind it she could hear other voices.

'Jessica! Jessica! Oh, if you can hear me, hurry! Please hurry.'

Jessie moved faster, holding the cloak tightly around her. She knew now where the call was coming from.

It was coming from the secret garden.

CHAPTER FOUR

'Where Am I?'

Holding her breath, Jessie pushed open the door in the hedge and stepped inside.

There was no one there. The scent of rosemary wafted about her as she stood motionless on the smooth grass. She took another step ...

Suddenly there was a sighing, whispering sound, a rush of air against her face, and a swirl of mist clouding her eyes. Jessie's cloak snapped away from her fingers. Her hair blew, crackling, around her head. She gasped with fear.

And then she was no longer in the secret garden. She was no longer anywhere at all she knew. And the voice was calling out in glee:

'We've got her! I told you so! I told you …' and then it broke off and cried out in surprise and horror. 'Oh, no! Oh no-o-o!'

Jessie gazed around her. She felt rather than saw that her cloak had slipped to the ground. Her hair was tangled on her shoulders. Far away she could hear singing.

She was standing on a pebbly road that ran beside a thick, dark hedge—a hedge much, much higher and stronger than the hedge of the secret garden, but marked all over with great grey patches of dead and dying wood. The air was sweet and shadowy. A memory stirred in her. Abruptly she looked up. There, sure enough, was a soft grey sky and, floating in it, a blue moon. But when she looked back at the hedge she could see no archway. There was no way she could tell how she had come through the hedge at all.

'This is a disaster!' snapped an angry voice.

Jessie spun around. Behind her, gaping at her in astonishment, were a fat little woman with eyes like black beads, her head wound up in a scarf; a thin, depressed-looking elf with long pointed ears that drooped at the tips; and a perfect miniature white horse with ribbons in its mane and a very cross expression on its face.

Jessie was astounded to realise that it was the horse who had spoken.

'A disaster!' it growled again. 'How could this have happened?' It rounded on the fat little woman. 'Patrice! I thought you said ...'

'This is definitely the Door,' the woman called Patrice fluttered. 'Maybelle, I promise you, it is *definitely*—'

'We're doomed!' wailed the elf. 'Doomed! Now we've used up all the magic. And the Door's shut again! And we still haven't found her. We got some human child instead. Oh, doom! Doom! Oh I *knew* this would never work. I knew it!'

Jessie covered her mouth with both hands to stop herself from screaming. Where was she? Who were these people?

There was a shout and a stomping sound in the distance.

'Look out!' hissed Maybelle, shaking her mane. 'The Royal Guard!'

'Oh, no!' squeaked the elf. He flapped his hands and began to run helplessly this way and that. 'Oh, what next? Now we're for it! Now we're for it!'

'Hide her, Patrice! Quick! Over there!' ordered Maybelle, ignoring him.

Patrice put her arm around Jessie and hustled

her away behind some nearby bushes. The noise of marching feet grew louder. With a last despairing squeak the elf leaped into the air and hung there, with his hands over his eyes.

Maybelle rolled her own eyes in disgust, then lowered her nose and began calmly to eat grass as if nothing at all unusual was happening.

'Stay still as still, dearie,' breathed Patrice in Jessie's ear.

Jessie had no intention of moving. She had never been so scared in her life. She huddled close to the ground, hardly daring to breathe.

In a few moments a group of soldiers in smart uniforms marched out of the dimness. Their booted feet scrunched on the pebbles of the roadway. Patrice squeezed Jessie's hand in her own small one. Jessie trembled and she closed her eyes. Her cloak was still lying where it had fallen on the road. The soldiers were certain to see it there as they walked past. Then they would know a stranger was here. And they would start to search. And then ...

'Halt!' The leading guard barked the order, and with a stamp the whole troop stopped dead, right in front of the spot where Jessie and Patrice were hiding.

'Five minutes' rest,' said the leading guard. The word was passed along the line, and one by one the guards thankfully broke away from the line and sat down on the grass. The leader glanced at the shivering elf in the air and snorted with tired amusement. She stretched her back and looked at the moon. 'It's midnight, Loris,' she said to the man next to her. 'The big day's come at last.'

'They're cutting it a bit fine if you ask me,' he answered gruffly. He flicked a finger at a bare patch in the dark, looming hedge. 'This won't last much longer. They say sunrise marks the fifty years exactly. The Lady came back last night, didn't she? Why hasn't she fixed up the magic by now? Why wait till the last minute?'

The leader shrugged. 'I suppose she knows what she's doing,' she replied. 'But I tell you what, I'll be glad to see the hedge back to normal again, Loris. It's dying fast. And without it we'll never keep the Others out. Too many of them.'

The man grunted his agreement. 'They say there are thousands of them, just waiting. They know the story. They've been hoping that the Lady won't come back. They've been hoping that the magic'll all run out, and the hedge'll die.' He jerked his head to where Maybelle was innocently grazing nearby. 'And you know what they'll do then,' he added grimly.

Maybelle raised her head and shook her white mane.

Behind the bushes, Jessie felt Patrice's hand tighten on her own.

'Sshh!' warned the leader. 'No point in getting creatures all upset. And anyhow, there's nothing to worry about, Loris. The Lady did come back, didn't she? Just like she said she would. And today's the day. Listen to those mermaids singing. They've gathered in the Bay. Hundreds of them. They know it's time. By morning the hedge'll be its old self again.'

'Lucky this magic business only happens once in a blue moon,' growled Loris. 'I don't like it.'

'Can't say I care for it much either,' grinned the leader. She pulled her cap straighter on her head. 'All right, Loris. They've had enough of a rest. Let's get going.'

Loris turned and shouted. Grumbling, the rest of the guards got up and formed into a line again.

'Forward!' barked the leader. And off the troop marched. Left, right, left, right, along the pebbled road. In a few moments everything was quiet again.

Carefully Patrice and Jessie clambered to their feet and crept out into the open. Jessie ran and picked up her cloak, which was still lying beside the hedge. It was a wonder that the guards hadn't noticed it, she thought. She hugged it to her for a moment. It was soft and warm, and smelled of home.

Maybelle trotted over to them. She glanced disdainfully up at the elf, who was still floating in the air, his hands firmly over his eyes.

'They've gone, Giff!' she called. 'Come down!'

But the elf didn't move.

'Giff!' the horse fumed. She turned to Patrice and pawed the ground. 'That fool of an elf,' she said through gritted teeth, 'is going to be the death of me.'

'He's probably blocked his ears as well as his eyes, poor thing,' said Patrice comfortably. 'He can't hear you.' She dug in her pocket and pulled out some round white sweets that smelled strongly of peppermint. 'Giff!' she shouted. Then, with expert aim, she sent a mint hurtling through the air, hitting the floating elf neatly on the back of the neck.

With a cry of fright Giff threw out his arms and legs, and fell to the ground with a thump. He lay on the grass, his ears quivering with fright. 'What hit me?' he quavered.

'Must have been a mosquito, dearie,' said Patrice mildly. 'Look, the guards have gone. Now we've got to go, too. It's not safe out here. We have to decide what we're going to do.'

Giff's ears drooped even more. He beat his fists on the grass. 'What's the point?' he wailed. 'The plan's in ruins. We failed. Completely, absolutely, utterly. We're doomed!'

'Well, if we're doomed,' snorted Maybelle, 'let's at least be doomed inside. Come on!'

Giff stumbled to his feet, sniffing, but Jessie stood her ground. She'd had enough of this. 'I'm not going anywhere until you tell me what's going on!' she said firmly. She turned to Maybelle. A horse she might be, but she definitely seemed to be the leader in this group.

'You tell me!' she demanded. 'Where am I? What is this place? And what's happening to the hedge that you need magic to fix? And who are the Others? How did I get here?' She took a deep breath. 'And the main thing is, how do I get back?'

CHAPTER FIVE

The Magic

Maybelle's eyelids fluttered. She tossed her mane uncomfortably. 'Ah … we'll go into all that later,' she said.

Jessie stamped her foot. 'No, we won't!' she insisted. 'We'll go into it now!'

Patrice gave a little cough. 'I really think we should tell the child everything, Maybelle,' she said. 'We owe her that much, don't you think?'

Maybelle humphed and tossed her mane again. 'All right,' she said finally. 'All right. But I insist that we go inside. The guards might be back this way, and we simply can't afford to be caught here with her.'

'The palace is just along the road a bit,' put in Patrice, tucking her arm through Jessie's. 'And a cup of hot chocolate wouldn't go astray, would it? We can talk on the way.'

Hot chocolate in a palace? Jessie looked at her in wonder. But Giff was licking his lips and Maybelle had already started trotting along the road, so she shrugged her shoulders and let Patrice lead her away.

'It's like this,' Patrice began, as they hurried along to catch up with Maybelle. 'This hedge, you see, is the border of the Realm. It keeps us safe from the Others.'

'Who—' began Jessie. Giff interrupted.

'Trolls!' he panted, his eyes wide with fright. 'Trolls and — ogres and — goblins — and dragons — and — giants — and — monsters — and — and —'

'And all sorts of nasties, dearie,' Patrice said, nodding. She sighed. 'They live in the Outlands, on the other side of the hedge.'

'But I thought *we* lived there,' said Jessie in surprise.

Patrice shook her head. 'Oh no, dearie,' she said. 'Yours is a quite different world. The Doors to your world open by magic. But the Outlands is part of *this* world. And the Outlands creatures would love to get into the Realm, my word they would. But they can't, you see? The hedge keeps them out.'

Ahead of them, Maybelle had slowed to a walk. As Jessie watched, she darted into a grove of tall, pale-leaved trees by the side of the road.

'Come on!' urged Patrice.

They followed Maybelle, and soon Jessie saw that behind the trees rose the turrets and spires of a great golden palace, just like the one in her grandfather's paintings. Light streamed from a vast doorway directly below a row of tall windows that stretched across the front of the palace. Jessie was filled with excitement. She imagined walking in that door like a princess and wished she was wearing proper clothes. A nightdress and bare feet didn't seem right for her first visit to a palace. She wondered if she should put on her cloak.

But to her disappointment the others ignored the main entrance. Instead, they slipped around the side of the building and led her to a very small door hidden behind some bushes.

'In here,' whispered Patrice, producing a key.

A few moments later they were in a narrow

hallway, and then a small, snug kitchen. Jessie looked around in surprise. 'Is this where they cook the food for the whole palace?' she asked.

Patrice burst out laughing, her little black eyes twinkling. 'Oh, hardly, dearie!' she giggled. 'The palace kitchens are a hundred times bigger than this. This is just for cooking my own meals in my time off. I'm the palace housekeeper, you know. Used to be nurse to all the palace babies when I was younger. Now, you sit down and I'll make you that hot chocolate.' She tied a white apron around her plump waist and began bustling around, getting chocolate and milk and cream, and putting cookies on a plate.

Everything seemed so ordinary that for a moment Jessie quite forgot that she was in a very strange place, with some very strange people, and that she had a lot of questions still to be answered. Then she caught sight of Maybelle leaning comfortably against the table with her back legs crossed, and remembered. 'Why do the ogres and trolls and things even *want* to get into your world?' she asked.

Maybelle gave a bitter snort. 'They're a nasty lot through and through, and they just want to destroy every beautiful thing they see,' she said.

'But apart from that, they want the gold that lies in our riverbeds. They're gold mad!' She sniffed. 'And of course,' she added casually, 'they want me.'

'You?' Jessie stared.

'Me, and all my friends and relations,' Maybelle said. 'They want to use us as slaves to work in their mines. In the dark, underground. Harnessed to carts full of rocks. Huh!' She lifted her head and stared straight ahead. Her words might sound disdainful, but Jessie could see that underneath she was afraid. She felt Patrice gripping her arm. The little woman was afraid, too.

'They won't get in, Maybelle,' quavered Giff. 'Will they?'

'If the hedge keeps going the way it is, I don't see how we can keep them out,' huffed the little horse.

'And that, dearie, is where you come in,' sighed Patrice, darting a look at Jessie as she put cups filled to the brim with foaming chocolate drink on the table. 'Or where you *would* have come in, if you were who we thought you were.'

'I don't understand!' cried Jessie.

'I'm not surprised,' snapped Maybelle. She heaved herself away from the table and glared at

Patrice. 'Let me tell it,' she ordered. She cleared her throat.

Jessie sipped her hot chocolate. It was delicious! She took another sip.

'The hedge that protects the Realm,' Maybelle began slowly and clearly, 'is very powerful. The evil creatures in the Outlands have their own magic. But it isn't strong enough to destroy the hedge. Except once in a blue moon. Every fifty years, to be exact.

'The hedge, you see, is kept strong by magic. It's the same magic that keeps the whole of the Realm running happily and smoothly. But every fifty years the magic runs out and has to be renewed. And this can only be done by the true Queen, using a spell that only she knows. If the magic isn't renewed, the hedge will crumble away.' Maybelle paused. 'Do you understand?' she asked abruptly.

Jessie nodded. 'Of course I do!' she exclaimed. 'And I suppose, from what the soldiers said, and because there's a blue moon in the sky, and because the hedge is dying, that the fifty years are nearly up now.'

Giff groaned and buried his nose in his cup. 'The mermaids are singing,' he whimpered. 'I don't know what they've got to sing about.'

'The mermaids always gather in the Bay for the renewal,' Patrice said, turning to Jessie. 'They always sing. They're singing now because they believe, like everyone else, that everything is going to be all right.'

'But you don't think so,' said Jessie, looking at their worried faces.

Maybelle shook her head slowly. 'Today at dawn it'll be fifty years exactly since the magic was last renewed. Only a few grains are left. There should be enough to last till daybreak. But even now ...'

'Oh!' cried Patrice, tearing off her apron and banging down her cup. 'Oh, I can't stand it! I have to go and see.'

'Me too, me too!' wailed Giff.

Maybelle snorted. 'We'll all go,' she said. 'May as well know the worst.' She jerked her head at Jessie. 'You come with us,' she said. 'We can't leave you here alone. Someone might come in.'

Jessie quickly finished her hot chocolate and then Patrice led the way from the kitchen, through her living room and out into a narrow corridor. The corridor led to some steep stairs, and then to yet another passageway that twisted and turned. The ceiling was very low. Jessie had to bend her head to follow the fat little woman toiling on ahead of her. Behind she could hear Giff panting and snuffling, and the neat clattering of Maybelle's hoofs on the floor.

They seemed to have been walking for a very long time when finally Patrice stopped. In front of them was what looked like a wooden wall. There was a narrow gap in the wall, from where a board was missing, and through it soft light streamed. Patrice turned and put her finger to her lips, then faced the front again and crept forward, very slowly. She knelt and looked through the hole. The others quickly joined her.

The other side of the wall was covered by a gauzy curtain, but Jessie could see easily through the fine material. She found that she was staring straight into a huge, magnificently decorated room lit with hundreds of candles. Crystal pillars rose, glittering, to the high ceiling. Great windows lined one wall. Jessie realised that these were the windows she had seen when she was looking at the front of the palace. In the middle of the room a beautiful, gentle-looking woman sat on a golden throne. Red hair streamed over her shoulders and down her back, and on her head she wore a silver crown. She seemed to be deep in thought.

Beside the throne a huge, strangely shaped crystal jar, open at the top and the bottom, hung suspended in the air, shining in the candlelight. It was empty except for a few flecks of gold drifting slowly around at the very top. As they watched, one golden fleck began to fall downwards. After a minute or two it slipped from the bottom of the jar, hung in the air for a brief moment, and then disappeared with a tiny flash. The woman on the throne sighed and looked even more worried than before.

The four friends pulled themselves away from the wall and crept a little way back down the corridor so they could talk. Patrice clasped her hands. Her eyes were bright with fear.

'Listen,' Jessie began. 'Why doesn't the Queen just fix the magic now? She's sitting right beside it. She could just say the spell and ...'

The other three shook their heads sadly. 'Poor Queen Helena can't do anything about it,' Patrice told her. 'She's not the true Queen. She's a dear, sweet lady, and she's ruled us well and wisely, hasn't she, Giff?'

Giff nodded violently. 'A bit soft-hearted, maybe,' he said.

Patrice shrugged. 'A bit too easily taken in by

rogues and scoundrels, that's true. But that hasn't mattered up to now.'

'Maybe not,' Maybelle rumbled. 'But in any case she's not the true Queen. She can't do a thing about the magic. She can't help at all.'

'Well, where *is* the true Queen, then?' demanded Jessie. 'Where is she? Why isn't she here?'

CHAPTER SIX

The Sisters

'll tell you the story,' said Maybelle. 'Sit down.'

Obediently, Jessie slid to the floor of the passageway and leaned against the wall. Giff and Patrice sat down beside her.

'Long ago,' Maybelle began, 'there were two little princesses in the Realm. One, the elder, would be Queen one day. It was she who learned from her mother the spell that would renew the magic. When the time came, only she would be able to make it work.

'She was beautiful, and wilful, and charming, and everyone loved her. Her younger sister,

Helena, was also beautiful and beloved. But she was altogether softer tempered and gentler. A good, obedient child.

'The little princesses grew up together in the palace with their cousin Valda, who was about the same age and looked very like them both. Valda always acted sweet and well behaved, but she had a cruel streak.' Maybelle wrinkled her nose. 'Valda was the sort of child who smiled at adults, but pinched and bullied smaller children when the adults weren't looking. You know what I mean.'

Jessie nodded. She'd met one or two children like that.

Maybelle went on. 'Despite their differences, the three girls played together, did their lessons together, and were like sisters. But all of them knew that Jessica would be Queen one day.'

Jessie jumped. 'What was that name?' she exclaimed.

Maybelle looked at her in surprise. 'Jessica,' she repeated. 'Our true Queen. The one we were calling when we got you by mistake. Anyway … when Jessica was sixteen, a stranger visited the Realm. He was tall and handsome— and from your world. He had found a Door, the same one you came through. There are many, if you know where to look.'

'He loved it here,' Giff put in, smiling sadly at the memory.

'So he did,' Maybelle said, nodding. 'He couldn't stay, because mortals can't survive in the Realm for long. But he visited us many times, over several years. He became friendly with many of the Folk. And every time he came, he went looking for Jessica.'

'Everyone could see that they were falling in love,' said Patrice, biting her lip. 'But no one thought there was any harm in it. No one saw the danger at first. And then—'

'They ran away together,' Jessie said slowly. 'He took her back to his own world and they got married. His name was Robert Belairs.'

They stared at her in surprise. 'How do you know that?' asked Giff fearfully.

'Please go on,' Jessie said to Maybelle. 'Tell me all of it.'

'They left on Jessica's twentieth birthday. The day that the magic was renewed by her mother, the Queen, and the blue moon hung in the sky,' said Maybelle, still looking at Jessie curiously. 'Jessica left a letter for her sister, Helena. She said that when the time came, Helena should rule the Realm in her place. She said that though she must now live in the new world she had chosen, she would not forget us.'

'She didn't take any of her beautiful clothes, or jewels, or anything,' sighed Patrice, wiping her eyes. 'She only took the charm bracelet that was hung with all her memories of home. In her letter to Helena she said she'd wear it always. It would stop her memory of the Realm from fading. It would help her to remember that in fifty years from that day she must come back—to renew the magic, anoint Helena's daughter as the next Queen, and keep the Realm safe.'

'Oh, there was terrible trouble when the King and Queen found out what had happened,' breathed Giff, his eyes wide.

'As you can imagine,' said Maybelle dryly. 'But eventually they calmed down and saw that what was done, was done. They issued a proclamation saying that when the time came, Helena should take the throne, as Jessica had asked. And that Helena's child would be Queen after her. Almost everyone thought they were right. The people loved Jessica and were sad that she was gone. But they loved Helena, too.'

'Valda wasn't happy, though,' interrupted Giff, shivering.

'No.' Patrice folded her arms and looked grim. 'Valda wasn't happy at all. Valda was very angry. She claimed that Jessica had disgraced the royal family by what she'd done. She said that as Helena was Jessica's sister, she was disgraced, too. And she said that Helena was weak and would bring the Realm to ruin.' She frowned. 'Ah, she was a nasty, jealous, spiteful piece, that Valda, even as a girl.'

'In a word,' Maybelle said impatiently, 'Valda said that she, Valda, should be anointed Queen in Helena's place. She gathered together some power-hungry, flattering creatures to support her. But she'd shown her true colours too soon. No one really wanted her as Queen.'

'Eventually, the King and Queen, and the people, too, lost patience with her. They warned her many times, but she wouldn't stop her troublemaking. Finally, a plot to take Helena's life was discovered. And that was the end. The Queen banished Valda to the Outlands. And she hasn't been heard of since.'

Patrice sighed. 'So now, instead of three princesses, there was only one. Poor Helena.

She was so lonely and afraid. She missed Jessica dreadfully. I remember it well. But in time she fell in love and was married, and took the throne. She had a child, a sweet girl, named Christie. And Helena has been a good Queen to us. A good and happy Queen. Now, though, she is in terrible trouble.'

'Jessica said she'd come back,' said Maybelle. 'But she hasn't. And now evil stalks the Realm. The Doors to your world have been locked. But Helena didn't lock them. Someone else did.'

'We three had to steal some of the last magic to force open the Door you came through,' whispered Patrice to Jessie, clasping and unclasping her hands. 'We were trying to call Jessica one last time. But she didn't come. I think … I think she must be dead.' Tears welled up in her eyes.

'No!' Jessie grabbed her arm. 'No, she isn't dead. She's at home. Jessica's my grandmother. The bracelet really must hold her memories of this place. Because she's lost it. And now she's forgotten what she has to do.' She spun around to face Maybelle. 'Quickly!' she rushed on. 'Get me home! I'll bring Jessica back to you.'

Maybelle shook her head. 'It's too late,' she said. 'You can't do anything now. And besides—'

'Jessica!' The cry from the throne room was startling in the silence. Then there were sharp, ringing footsteps on the marble floor, and a tinkling sound that Jessie recognised.

The friends scuttled back along the passage to the curtained wall and peeped into the room beyond. Queen Helena had jumped to her feet and was facing someone they couldn't see. 'Oh, Jessica,' she was crying. 'The magic is ebbing so fast, so fast! It is past midnight. The hedge is dying every moment you delay. And my guards say thousands of trolls are massing on the other side. Our people are becoming afraid. Please, please renew the magic now.'

'Oh, the morning will be time enough, dear Helena,' yawned another voice. 'We have until dawn, after all. Just now I am tired to death. A relaxing bath and a soft bed are all I am planning on for the next few hours.' There was a low laugh, and then a woman walked into view.

Jessie gasped.

The woman was small, and beautiful like Helena, with long, golden-red hair. She looked very like one of the great ladies in Robert Belairs' paintings. But her eyes were as cold as green ice, and her mouth was thin and proud. On her shoulder perched a pretty grey kitten that Jessie had seen before. And on her wrist was a bracelet. A charm bracelet, which tinkled as she looked around her, smiling at the room as though she owned it.

'Granny's bracelet!' breathed Jessie. 'That woman's got Granny's bracelet!' She made a move to spring through the curtain, but Giff gasped in horror and Patrice grabbed her arm and held her back.

'Be still! Be quiet! She mustn't know you're here!' she hissed, pulling Jessie away from the curtain. 'Or you'll disappear, as other people have.' She tugged until Jessie moved with her and the others further down the passageway.

When they were far enough away not to be overheard, Jessie twisted around to face them. 'Why does Queen Helena call that woman Jessica?' she demanded.

Maybelle curled her lip. 'Because that woman says she's Jessica,' she snorted. 'And Helena believes her, as do most others here. Because she looks like Jessica. Because she came into the Realm at the right time. And because she's wearing Jessica's bracelet. To most people, the bracelet is proof of her identity.'

'She stole the bracelet,' exclaimed Jessie. 'Or rather, her horrible cat stole it for her. He tripped Granny up and made her hurt her wrist so the bracelet had to be taken off. Then he took it and hid it, and waited till he got the chance to move it out of the house. I realise now. I actually saw him carrying it to the secret garden late last night. He was taking it back through the Door, to that woman, so she could pretend to be Granny.' She turned to Maybelle. 'But who is she?' she urged. 'Why is she doing this?'

'We believe she's Valda,' said Maybelle. Giff and Patrice nodded solemnly.

'We believe that for all these years of her exile she's been building her power, making her own evil magic, and planning her revenge,' the little horse went on. 'And now, when the Realm is at its weakest, she's returned to carry out her plan. She stole Jessica's bracelet to take away her Realm memories. And she used her own magic to lock the Doors, in case we tried to bring Jessica back ourselves. Jessica could undo her lock-spell in a moment. But we can't. Not without magic.'

She sighed. 'But why Valda's pretending to be Jessica, and why she claims she's going to renew the magic, when she knows she can't do it, we don't know. After all, she can't pretend she's Jessica forever. She *can't* renew the magic. In the end, everyone will find out that she's an imposter.'

'The trouble is, by then the magic will be gone,' muttered Patrice.

'Send me back!' cried Jessie. 'Send me back quickly, and I'll bring the real Jessica to you. I will!'

They all looked at her sadly. 'We can't,' said Maybelle simply. 'The Door is locked, and we don't have the magic to open it any more. We're very sorry. But we can't send you back. Ever.'

CHAPTER SEVEN

Jessie's Plan

Later, Jessie couldn't remember how she'd got back to Patrice's cosy little kitchen. All she remembered was finding herself sitting at the table and crying, while Giff forlornly patted her arm and Patrice fussed around offering her cakes and drinks she couldn't swallow.

Maybelle stood shaking her head. 'Sorry,' she kept saying. 'Very sorry.'

'Sorry!' choked Jessie at last. She gave a shuddering sob. 'What good's that? I want to go home!' She wiped her eyes with the back of her hand. Giff tremblingly offered her a green-and-white spotted handkerchief, and she took it. 'I want to go home,' she repeated more firmly.

Patrice clasped her little brown hands. 'Oh, we wish we could help,' she cried. 'We'd do anything to help if we could.'

'If only the real Jessica was here,' moaned Giff, his drooping ears quivering. 'Jessica would know what to do. Jessica would do something. Oh dear, oh dear!'

Jessie looked up. A memory stirred in her mind. She remembered her grandmother's laughing face and her voice: *Don't worry so. All will be well.* They were right. Granny wouldn't have given up. She lifted her chin.

'Well, *I'm* here,' she said. 'And I'm Jessica's grand-daughter.' Then she thought of something else. Some other words, spoken in her mother's calm, practical voice: *What we need round here is some common sense.* She raised her head higher. 'I'm Jessica's grand-daughter,' she said, 'and I'm Rosemary's daughter, too. And I'm not going to let any nasty old witch take over this place. Or steal my Granny's memory. *Or* stop me from getting home. I'm going to *make* her open the Door for me. And that's that!'

Giff stared at her admiringly.

'Oh, that's the way!' shrilled Patrice. 'Oh, she does remind me of Jessica, Maybelle.'

'That's as may be,' retorted Maybelle. 'But it's not as easy as all that. What exactly are you going to do, child, may I ask?'

The others waited expectantly.

'Well ...' Jessie hesitated. Of course she hadn't the faintest idea. She shivered.

'You're cold!' exclaimed Patrice instantly. 'Oh dear. I'll light a fire. And in the meantime ...' She looked around and spied the old grey cloak lying on a chair by the door. She picked it up and handed it to Jessie. 'Here,' she said. 'Put this on, dearie.'

Thankfully, Jessie wrapped the cloak around her. Again she breathed in its warm, homey smell.

And then Giff screamed.

Jessie stared at him in surprise. The little elf was as pale as chalk. He was pointing at her with a shaking finger.

'What's the matter?' she asked.

'It's the cloak,' exclaimed Patrice, goggle-eyed. 'That's what it is! Giff, stop that noise, for goodness sake! You're making my head spin!'

Maybelle moved away from her place in the corner and approached Jessie cautiously. She lifted her lips, felt carefully around, and then pulled at the cloak with her teeth until it fell away from Jessie's shoulders.

Patrice clapped her hands. 'Told you!' she shrieked delightedly.

'Did you get this from your grandmother, child?' asked Maybelle, dropping the cloak to the ground.

'My name's Jessie!' Jessie snapped, feeling very ruffled. 'And yes, it belongs to Granny. But why did you pull it off?'

'Because it makes you invisible, dearie,' giggled Patrice. 'You gave us such a fright. Didn't you know?'

Jessie stared. 'No,' she said blankly. 'Invisible? But that's not true, Patrice. I wear it all the time at Blue Moon—I mean, at Granny's place. And there's no way it makes me invisible there.'

'Well, it does here,' said Maybelle with excitement. She pushed at the cloak with her nose. 'My word, a cloak of invisibility! I haven't seen one of these for years.'

'Only the royal family have them, Maybelle,' said Patrice primly. She gathered the cloak up in her arms and smoothed its folds before handing it back to Jessie with a look of respect in her eyes.

Jessie stared at the soft grey material. Invisible! The word rang in her head. 'Do you know where in the palace Valda is staying?' she asked suddenly.

Patrice nodded. 'Of course. In Jessica's old bedroom,' she said.

'Take me there, then,' urged Jessie. 'Come on! I've got a plan. I'll explain it to you as we go.'

A guard stood outside the bedroom door. The four friends peeped at him cautiously from their hiding place behind a golden statue that stood in a turning of the passageway.

'What if she's already had her bath?' whispered Patrice. 'It's late. She might already be in bed.'

'Then we'll have to play it by ear,' Jessie whispered back. 'Don't worry!' She pulled Granny's cloak around her shoulders and watched as the others blinked. She really was invisible! 'Are you sure you want to go through with this?' she asked. 'It'll mean trouble for you—afterwards.'

'Of course we're sure,' Patrice said, nodding. 'Let's go.'

'Good luck!' added Maybelle.

Giff waggled his ears and patted the air where he thought Jessie might have been.

With a wave that of course Giff and Maybelle couldn't see, Jessie slipped from behind the statue and, with Patrice beside her, walked up the corridor towards the guard. Patrice's shoes clattered on the polished marble floor. Jessie's bare feet made no sound at all. The guard stood staring straight ahead, unblinking and at attention, as they reached his side.

'The Lady will be wanting these,' Patrice said to the guard. She showed him the two fluffy white towels she carried in her arms. He nodded and knocked at the door.

'Yes?' called a proud voice.

The guard winked at Patrice and opened the door. Patrice bustled into the room beyond, the invisible Jessie close behind her.

The walls of the bedroom were hung with pale blue curtains that fell to the floor in silky folds. The carpet was white and deliciously soft under Jessie's bare toes. The bedhead was painted with tiny blue and gold flowers to match the bed's silken spread. Through an open door a white marble bathroom could be seen. Jessie looked around her in wonder. It was hard to believe that this was where her grandmother had slept when she was a girl. It really was a room fit for a princess.

The woman they had seen in the throne room was standing in front of a tall mirror in the centre of the room. Her red hair hung like a gleaming shawl down her back, and she was wearing a deep purple robe. The grey kitten sat at her feet.

'I brought you some fresh towels, my lady,' said Patrice, dropping a deep curtsy.

'I already have towels, Patrice,' said the woman coldly. 'I had to ask for them earlier. Some silly girl brought them to me. It seemed you couldn't be found.'

Patrice bowed her head. 'It is my rest day today, my lady,' she said.

'Rest day?' The woman's lips curved in a thin smile. 'It seems you have all been spoiled while I have been away.' She raised her hands to her hair and the charm bracelet on her wrist tinkled. 'Helena is a dear girl, but far too soft. We shall see about all that—later.'

'Yes, my lady,' murmured Patrice, and bobbed another curtsy.

The woman's smile faded. She turned to face Patrice. 'Don't think you can fool me with your curtsies and your "my ladys", Patrice,' she sneered. 'I know that you have been trying to cause trouble. You and that creature Maybelle, and the absurd Giff. I have … friends … who tell me what is going on in the palace.'

'Spies, you mean,' flashed Patrice, gripping the towels in her arms while her face blushed red.

'Friends,' snapped the woman. 'Loyal subjects who are pleased to have their true Queen home again.'

'You aren't our true Queen,' Patrice burst out. 'You might fool everyone else, but you don't fool me. You aren't Jessica!'

In the corner Jessie put her hand over her mouth. Oh, not now! Oh, be careful, Patrice, she begged silently.

But the woman in front of the mirror only threw back her head and laughed. 'You poor, silly creature. Who am I then?'

'You're Valda,' cried Patrice. 'I didn't nurse you, Jessica and Helena as babies for nothing. I'd know each one of you if I hadn't seen you for a hundred years. You were mean, spiteful and jealous as a child, Valda, and so you are now.' The little servant was shaking with fear, but she stood up proudly.

Valda narrowed her eyes. 'You never liked me,

Patrice,' she spat. 'Never! And I didn't like you.' She took a step forward, her fist raised. 'You say one word to anyone about this and you'll regret it. You'll regret it till the end of your days. Now get out! *Get out!*'

Patrice scuttled to the door, the towels still clutched in her arms. As she left the room she glanced back once, her small black eyes despairing.

Don't worry, Patrice, thought Jessie grimly. We're going to defeat her. And it's now or never.

CHAPTER EIGHT

The Thief

When the door closed again and Valda believed herself to be alone, she turned back to the mirror and touched a finger to her smooth cheek. The grey kitten twined itself about her feet. She smiled.

'When morning comes, my little friend,' she murmured to it, 'these fools will pay for their treatment of me, for I will be Queen indeed. Jessica lies helpless in the mortal world, with no memory of the Realm. She will not stir to save her people now. The removal of the bracelet has seen to that. A few more hours and the last magic will have gone. The hedge will crumble. And my army from the Outlands will come in. Then the people of the Realm will see what it is to be ruled. They will learn to do exactly what they're told. Or face the consequences.'

She smiled again, then turned and went towards the bathroom. Jessie held her breath, her ears straining. She heard the sounds of water running in the marble tub and Valda moving around. She heard the rustle of satin as the purple robe was tossed carelessly to the floor, and the clatter of slippers kicked aside. And then she heard the sound she had been waiting for. The tiny jingling of the charm bracelet as Valda removed it and put it down on the side of the bath before getting into the water. Jessie's heart leaped. She'd been certain that the bath would be the one place where Valda could not keep the bracelet on her wrist. And she'd been right.

Jessie stole to the bathroom door. Valda was lying in a billowing mass of scented, pale blue bubbles. Her hair was wound up in a white towel, her eyes were closed. The charm bracelet lay close beside her shoulder. Jessie held her breath and moved into the room. The white floor was cold and smooth under her feet. She made no sound.

Valda lay still. Jessie stretched out her hand for the bracelet. She took it between two fingers, and began to ease it towards her. And then she snatched it, jingling, from the edge of the bath, and ran for the door.

Valda's eyes flew open. She screamed with rage and grasped the slippery sides of the bath, struggling to get up.

'You're too late!' cried Jessie. 'I've got Jessica's bracelet. I'm going to take it back to her, so her memory of the Realm will come back. And you can't stop me!' She threw open the bedroom door and darted out into the hallway. The guard on duty, flabbergasted, looked wildly right and left. He could hear Valda's shrieks of rage. He could hear Jessie's thudding footfalls and the tinkling of the bracelet. But he could see nothing at all.

Jessie pounded on, following the way Patrice had shown her. Sleepy guards and servants spun around gasping as they felt and heard her pass, then jumped as they became aware of Valda's furious shouting in the distance: 'Stop her! Stop her!'

Panting, Jessie raced down the wide stairs that led to the ground floor and the main entrance. She could hear heavy feet coming after her now.

The great golden doors were standing open. She began to run for them.

'Bar the doors! Quickly! Quickly!' shrilled Valda from the head of the stairs. Jessie glanced behind and saw her stamping in fury, wrapped in her purple robe, her red hair streaming. Dozens of soldiers and servants were thundering around her and down the stairs, running to catch the invisible thief. The guards at the entrance jumped to attention and started to swing the heavy doors shut.

But Jessie was too fast for them. She darted forward and just managed to dash between the doors as they closed. She glimpsed the startled eyes of one guard as he heard her pass. Then she was out in the open air and the doors were crashing shut behind her, and Valda was screaming in rage, 'You fools! You fools!'

❦

Five minutes later, outside the Door where they had first met Jessie, Maybelle raised her head. She heard shouting and the sounds of many running feet, mingled with the distant music of mermaids' song. 'Here we go,' she said to herself. She lowered her head and began quietly nibbling the grass.

In moments the darkened roadway was alive with lights and people. Valda, purple robe flying, swept along at the head of the Royal Guard, the grey kitten perched on her shoulder. When she saw Maybelle she gasped, then frowned in deadly anger.

'You!' she breathed. 'I might have known you'd be mixed up in this.' She pointed a trembling finger at Maybelle. 'All right! Where is the thief hiding?'

Maybelle raised her head and carefully licked up a piece of grass that was stuck to her bottom lip. 'I beg your pardon?' she mumbled, her mouth full.

'Tell me!' Valda ordered. 'Or it will be the worse for you!'

Maybelle twitched her ears. 'I heard a jingling sound running past me and off up the road a few minutes ago,' she said, turning her head to look to the left. 'Someone was in an awful hurry. Running so fast I couldn't even see who it was.'

'You're lying!' Spitting with rage, Valda whirled around to face the gaping soldiers. 'Search!' she commanded. 'The thief must be around here somewhere!'

'You're wasting your time,' said Maybelle calmly. She crossed her front hoofs and watched with interest as the guards began stamping around the area.

Suddenly there was a pounce, a squeak and a cry of triumph. The guard Loris ran up to Valda, carrying a small, struggling figure under his arm.

'Ah ...' hissed Valda. 'Giff the elf. Giff the coward. And what are you doing out here so late, may I ask?'

'He was hiding in a tree, my lady,' growled Loris, holding Giff out to show her. Giff trembled and chattered with fright.

'Tell me, Giff,' cooed Valda, her eyes as cold as green glass, 'do you know anything about a thief?'

Giff jumped and squirmed in Loris' hand. His terrified eyes were fixed on Valda's.

'Speak!' snarled Valda. 'And speak now. And then I may, I just may, spare your miserable life! If not ...'

'No!' squeaked Giff. 'No, don't hurt me, please. I'll tell! I'll tell!'

Maybelle snorted warningly.

'Ignore the horse,' sneered Valda, still holding Giff's gaze. 'She can't help you. No one can help you. You know where the thief is, don't you, elf? And you're going to tell me. Otherwise … !'

Giff covered his eyes with his hands and burst into tears. 'She went through the Door!' he sobbed. 'She had magic. She went through the Door!'

'What?' Valda wheeled around to face the hedge, her face a mask of baffled rage.

'Magic? But how … ?' She glared at Maybelle. 'You thought you'd gain extra time for your sneaking thief by sending us off on a wild-goose chase, didn't you?' she shouted. 'You lying creature! You … !'

She pointed at the hedge. 'Open!' she screamed. There was a sighing sound and a gust of cold air. And then, in the centre of the hedge, an arched door appeared, shimmering and black.

'Go,' said Valda to the kitten on her shoulder. 'Bring the bracelet back to me. Do not fail!'

The creature sprang, hissing, from her shoulder and ran for the Door. It leaped into the blackness with a yowl.

Valda turned back to Maybelle. 'So your plan to deceive me failed,' she snarled. 'Guards! Tether this horse and take it back to the palace. In the morning we will decide what its fate will be. The elf, too. Put it in chains!'

The guards looked at one another. Some of them weren't sure they liked this so-called Queen. They didn't like her frowns, or her cruelty, or her shouted orders. They didn't understand what was going on.

'Obey!' shrilled Valda. She watched as the guards slowly and sullenly did as she asked. She knew they were unhappy. But that didn't matter to her. In the morning she would have a proper troop of soldiers: the trolls and ogres who had sworn to obey her in return for gaining entrance to the Realm.

She frowned slightly at the thought of the stolen bracelet. How had the thief obtained a cloak of invisibility? How had the thief managed to open the Door? 'Jessica!' Valda said to herself, and her frown deepened. She had thought that she had taken care of Jessica.

Then she raised her head. There was no need to worry. Soon it would be dawn. Then the Realm would be lost to Jessica and her kind forever. Valda smiled. She was too strong and too clever to be defeated now. Look how she had forced that stupid elf to tell her where the thief had gone.

Maybelle, tethered tightly and being led away between two guards, saw the smile. And despite her own trouble, and the pain of the ropes on her neck, she allowed herself a small smile, too.

She remembered Jessie's words as they had hurried through the palace hallways. 'Once I've got the bracelet, we'll have to make Valda open the Door so I can get back to Granny,' she had said. 'And the only way she'll do that is if she thinks I've gone through first.'

'How do we make her think that?' Maybelle had asked. 'She'll never believe us if we tell her.'

Jessie had laughed. 'No,' she'd said. 'But if she thinks she's *forced* someone to tell her, she'll believe, won't she?'

And then she'd turned to Giff and told him what she wanted him to do.

How angry Valda would be if she knew how she had been tricked. How angry if she had heard, as Maybelle had, the tiny tinkle of the charm bracelet as Jessie followed Valda's grey kitten through the Door that Valda herself had opened.

Maybelle plodded on. Good luck, Jessie, she thought. Good luck—and please hurry!

CHAPTER NINE

Panic!

Jessie ran from the secret garden, the bracelet clutched in her hand. The night was dark and cool, but she didn't think of that. All she thought of was reaching the house, of waking her grandmother, of giving her back the bracelet so her memory would return. Then Granny could get back to the Realm in time to renew the magic.

She saw that the back door of Blue Moon was still open, and saw the shadow of Flynn standing guard. She was nearly there—

And then, like a grey streak, Valda's creature was flying from the trees, tangling in her legs, and Jessie was falling heavily onto the grass, her cloak twisting around her. And the creature was tearing at her hand with its claws, hissing and spitting, trying to make her give up the bracelet. It wasn't pretending to be a cute and helpless kitten now. It was showing its terrible strength.

'No!' shrieked Jessie desperately. 'No!'

Flynn's growl was like rumbling thunder as he sprang. In a single bound he leaped from the doorstep to where Jessie had fallen. And then he was snarling at Valda's creature and beating it back, driving it away into the trees.

Jessie stumbled to her feet. Her wrist and the back of her hand were torn and bleeding, but she still had the bracelet. Behind her she could hear the two animals hissing and fighting. She didn't look back: she knew that Flynn could take care of himself. Her job was to give the bracelet to her grandmother.

The house was very still. Jessie crept to Granny's room and pushed the door open.

'Who is it?' asked a trembling voice. Granny was awake!

Jessie switched on the light. Her grandmother lay in bed, looking very small and pale, her white hair streaming over her shoulders and onto the covers.

'It's only me,' whispered Jessie. She ran over to the bed and held out the charm bracelet. 'Granny, I've found your bracelet.'

'I couldn't sleep,' mumbled the old lady. 'There's something ... I know there's something I've forgotten. Very important. So important. But I can't think what it is.' She tossed her head on the pillows.

Jessie took Granny's unbandaged wrist gently in her hands. She fastened the bracelet around it with shaking fingers, then stood back.

Her grandmother looked at her for a long moment, and then in her eyes Jessie saw a spark, a light that grew and grew in strength. Granny gasped and struggled up on her pillows. 'The Realm!' she panted. 'My birthday!' She clasped Jessie's arm. 'I ... I have to get back to the Realm! Jessie ... I have to renew the magic.'

'I know,' whispered Jessie. She tugged at her grandmother's arm. 'Granny, come with me now. We haven't much time. Valda is in the Realm, and everyone thinks she's you! She's planning to let the hedge die. And Maybelle, Patrice and Giff are in such trouble! You can save them! Oh, please come now. To the Door in the secret garden!'

Her grandmother threw aside the covers and

tried desperately to push herself from the bed. But she was so weak! Jessie's heart sank. How would she ever walk all the way down to the secret garden?

Through the window she could see the sky was growing paler. It was nearly dawn!

'We have to hurry!' she said urgently. She put her arms around Granny's shoulders and tried to help her. But when the old woman was finally standing on the floor, Jessie realised it was hopeless. Her grandmother had been in bed too long, and was too frail to make the walk. Gently she pushed her back onto the bed.

'We have to find another way,' she said.

Granny looked at her in despair. 'I must find a Door,' she breathed. 'Another Door.' She lifted her hand to her forehead and the bracelet jingled on her wrist. 'I'm still ... I can't quite remember everything,' she said. 'But I'm sure ... I'm sure there was another way. I'm sure Robert said ...'

Jessie's heart leaped. 'Yes!' she exclaimed. 'Wait, Granny. I know. I know!'

She left her grandmother sitting staring after her and rushed from the room, the grey cloak flying behind her. Quietly, quietly, she told herself. If Mum wakes up we'll never be able to explain in time.

She ran on tiptoe to the studio. The painting

was standing where she had last seen it. As she picked it up she saw again the card on the back. *For my princess on her birthday. Better to be safe than sorry. All my love, always, Robert.*

Good, careful, practical Robert Belairs. The man who had fallen in love with a fairy princess, but always kept his feet on the ground. Robert had always believed in preparing for the worst. Before he died, he had made for his princess a painting that was a spare key to her old home.

Jessie staggered through the shadowy corridors of Blue Moon, the painting clutched firmly in her arms. It was heavy, and her injured hand hurt. But she didn't stop until she'd reached her grandmother's room again and had put the painting on the floor.

As her grandmother stared at it, another veil of confusion and forgetfulness lifted from her eyes. She smiled. 'Robert!' she breathed, her voice full of love. She reached for Jessie's hand. 'I must go,' she said.

'Take me with you,' urged Jessie. 'You need help. I'll help you.'

Granny squeezed her fingers. 'Leave on the cloak, then,' she said. 'So Valda will not see you. Are you ready?'

Jessie nodded. She saw her grandmother's green eyes flash. 'Open!' said a voice she hardly recognised. And then Granny was gripping her hand even more tightly, and Jessie was shivering in a breath of cool wind. The archway in the painting seemed to grow larger and larger, until it was filling all her sight …

And then they were no longer in the bedroom at Blue Moon. They were somewhere else. Not on the roadway beside the dying hedge, where the dawn was staining the sky golden pink and the blue moon was setting. Not in the forest, where the pale-leaved trees rustled their fear in the mauve light. Not in front of the golden palace, where a crowd of anxious people—fairies, elves, gnomes, pixies, creatures of every shape and sort—had gathered, waiting. But in the throne room, under the light of a thousand candles. Beside the twinkling crystal jar, where one last gold fleck drifted slowly downwards.

'What is the meaning of this?' thundered a voice.

Jessie spun around. In an instant her gaze took in the people around her. Queen Helena, looking terrified, stood with her daughter, Christie. A crowd of guards and finely dressed fairy folk, serious-faced dwarves, elves and pixies, huddled behind her. And in one corner of the room were the bowed figures of Patrice, Maybelle and Giff, wound round with chains.

But right in the centre of the huge room stood another figure. A figure wearing a dress of deepest blue and a crown of gold. Valda. Valda, frowning thunderously, pointing at the frail elderly woman standing motionless and apparently alone, her hand on the crystal jar.

'Who is this old crone who dares to break into my palace!' she shrieked. Her eyes widened. 'She is wearing my bracelet!' she choked. 'The thief!' She whirled around to face the guards. 'Take her away!' she ordered.

The guards hesitated.

'What are you waiting for!' screamed Valda. 'Are you afraid? Of a silly old woman? Of a nobody, alone and unprotected? Take her away! I command you!'

Two of the guards reluctantly stepped forward.

Jessie glanced at her grandmother in panic. Her head was bent. The hand that rested on the crystal jar was trembling. Granny needed time. Jessie untied the ribbons that held the cloak around her neck. The cloak dropped to the floor.

The people gasped as she appeared before their eyes.

'She's not alone!' shouted Jessie. 'And she isn't a nobody! She's …'

'Jessica!' The cry echoed through the room. And Patrice was staggering forward, pulling at the chains that bound her, her eyes streaming with tears. 'Jessica!'

A great shout rose up from the crowd. The guards fell back. Helena stood as if frozen, her hands pressed to her mouth.

'Absurd!' shrilled Valda. 'I am Jessica!' But her voice was full of dread as well as anger.

Jessie glanced fearfully at her grandmother. Granny's eyes were fixed on the last fleck of gold as it drifted slowly, slowly downwards. When it reached the bottom of the jar it would float out into the air and disappear. And then …

'Granny, the spell,' Jessie urged her. 'The words! Say the words!'

Her grandmother turned her head and looked at Jessie. 'If only I had more time,' she said, her voice very low. 'More memories are coming back to me every second. But the words … Jessie, I can't remember the words!'

CHAPTER TEN

'Remember ...'

She's a fraud!' screeched Valda, her eyes fixed greedily on the drifting gold speck. It had nearly reached the bottom of the jar now. 'A thief and a fraud! And if you won't remove her from this chamber, I will!' She strode across the room towards Jessica, her hands, tipped with long, pointed nails, outstretched.

'No!' cried Helena. She sprang and caught Valda around the waist. Valda turned, hissing, and tried to push her away. 'Jessica!' sobbed Helena. 'Oh, my Queen, my sister! Help us!'

At the sound of her sister's voice, Granny's green eyes flashed with memory. The bracelet tinkled on her wrist as she stretched out her hand again and began to move it over the crystal. Then softly, softly, she began to sing, a strange, lilting song with words that didn't rhyme: 'Blue moon floating, mermaids singing, elves and pixies, tiny horses, dwarves and fairies ...'

Jessie's heart lurched. She was the only one close enough to hear the words. And she knew them! These were the words she'd heard so often when Granny sang to her at night. For all these years, Granny had been singing the spell!

Granny took a deep breath and closed her eyes. She wasn't sure what came next! Jessie put her arm around her and leaned forward till her lips touched her grandmother's ear: 'Wait together, in the silence,' she breathed.

Granny's eyes opened again. And this time they were full of light. 'Wait together, in the silence,' she sang, 'waiting for the magic rain. Come down, come down, come down and gather, I the Queen command it now!'

There was a moment's electric silence. Then, without a sound, the last gold fleck drifted from the crystal jar. It hung in the air, winking, in its last instant of life.

Valda shrieked with triumph. Helena screamed

and hugged Christie tight. The candles flickered and dimmed ...

And then the room blazed. Blazed with golden light. And the crystal jar was twisting and turning in the air, filling to overflowing with millions upon millions of chips of solid sunshine that sprayed out and over the top and showered the amazed people with glittering glory. The gold shot up to the ceiling and beat against the windows like sparks from a thousand fireworks.

In the centre of the shimmering, whirling mass of gold stood Jessica. But no longer was she frail and old. Now she was again the Jessica of the paintings—young, lovely and triumphant, holding up her arms, shaking back thick, long hair that was no longer white, but shining red.

Jessie blinked, laughed, stared in amazement, hugged herself with relief. With overwhelming happiness she heard a great roar rising up from the crowd outside the palace, as the people saw the dazzling light, and broadly smiling guards swung open the windows to let their cheering in.

With a cry of rage, Valda made a dash for the door. But a row of guards stepped forward to block her way. She spun around and shouted to Jessica.

'Queen Jessica, I am your cousin! Do not harm me. Let me go!'

Jessica stepped forward. 'You are my cousin, Valda,' she said gravely. 'But you are my enemy, too. My enemy, and the enemy of all the Realm.' She sighed. 'We will not harm you. That is your way, but not ours. We will simply again put you out of our sight.' She lifted her hand. 'By my power as Queen, in the time of renewal of the magic,' she said, 'I banish you once more to the Outlands. This time, the magic will hold. Now, go!' She pointed a stern finger. And with a final shriek, Valda dissolved before their eyes and disappeared into the air.

An hour later, Jessie and her grandmother stood by the hedge, which stretched high and glossy green before them. On one side of them stood Helena and her daughter, Christie, and on the other stood Patrice, Maybelle and Giff.

'Oh, Jessica, why won't you stay!' begged Helena, with tears in her beautiful eyes. 'This is your home! We need you!'

Jessica shook her head. 'No,' she smiled. 'My home is in the world of mortals now. I made that choice long ago, Helena, and I don't regret it. It's brought me so much happiness.' She laid her hand on Jessie's arm.

'And you don't need me, Helena,' she went on, gently. 'You'll go on ruling the Realm as well as ever. And only half an hour ago you saw me anoint Christie as the Queen to come after you. You know I've taught her the words to renew the magic when her turn comes.' She smiled at the girl, who smiled shyly back. 'So the burden has been lifted from my shoulders, and the future of the Realm is secure.'

'You will come and visit, though, won't you?' pleaded Giff. 'You or Jessie. Please?'

'Oh, please!' echoed Patrice.

'It might be just as well,' Maybelle put in gruffly. She coughed. 'For a human, the girl seems to be rather useful.'

Jessica smiled again. 'Ah well,' she said. 'We'll see. I feel it would be best for me to keep away. But Jessie's a different matter. And if she wants to, and you're willing ...'

Helena stepped forward and pressed something into Jessie's hand. 'You have done us a great service, Jessie,' she said. 'We give you this as a token of our love and thanks.'

Jessie looked. In her hand was a chain bracelet. A single golden charm hung from it. A heart.

'Every time you visit us,' said Helena, 'another charm will be added. And this way you will always remember us. The Doors are all open again now, my dear. You will always be welcome. You have only to wish.'

Jessica's green eyes warmed as she fastened the bracelet on her grand-daughter's wrist. 'Jessie will be back,' she said. 'Oh, yes.'

The sisters and friends hugged and kissed each other. Giff was crying openly, and even Maybelle was seen to snort away a tear or two. Then Jessica turned towards the Door. 'Open!' she said. The archway appeared, and with a rushing sound she and her grand-daughter moved through it to the other side.

❦

Rosemary stepped through the doorway into the secret garden. She gasped. Her mother and her daughter were standing there in the centre of the lawn, bathed in sunlight. She rubbed her dazzled eyes. For a moment, just for a moment, her mother's long, flowing hair had looked as bright and red as Jessie's. But when she looked again, of course, Jessica's hair was quite white. It must have been a trick of the sunlight, she thought.

'Mum! Jessie! I was so worried about you!' she exclaimed. 'Neither of you were in your beds! What possessed you to come out so early? Jessie, Granny should be resting.'

'Oh no, Rosemary darling,' smiled Granny. 'Today's my birthday! And I'm much better now. So much better.'

They began walking back to the house. 'Mum, you're ... you're walking so well! And you've found your bracelet,' said Rosemary, noticing the bright gold on her mother's wrist.

'Jessie found it for me,' laughed Granny. 'And now she's got one of her own.'

Rosemary looked at her shrewdly. 'Something's happened, hasn't it, Mum?' she said. 'You've got that look in your eye like you used to have when I was little.'

The charm bracelet tinkled on Granny's wrist. She looked around and sighed contentedly, breathing in the sweet mountain air. 'It's a beautiful, beautiful day,' she said.

Rosemary stopped. 'You're not going to move to town and live with us, Mum, are you?' she said suddenly.

'No, darling,' Granny answered. 'I'm better here. But I've been thinking. Instead of me coming to live with you, you and Jessie could …'

'Oh no!' laughed Rosemary, holding up her hand. 'Oh no. We can't move! What about my job? And Jessie's school? What about …?'

'Nurse Allie said there were several jobs for nurses at the hospital here,' said Granny. 'Good jobs.'

'And there's a school here,' Jessie put in eagerly. 'A good school.'

Rosemary regarded them both helplessly. 'I'll think about it,' she said at last.

Jessie and her grandmother exchanged happy looks. They both knew what her decision would be.

'This has been a wonderful birthday morning,' said Granny. 'I'll never forget it.' She smiled and tapped her bracelet. 'Now, I'll never forget it.'

Jessie looked at her own bracelet, shining gold against her tanned wrist. 'No,' she said, thinking of all she'd done and seen, and of all the adventures still to come. 'Neither will I.'

Goosebumps

SAY CHEESE AND DIE!

Once again, Greg found himself thinking of the pictures he had taken with the weird camera.

First Michael. Then Terry. Then Bird. Then his father.

All four photos had shown something terrible that hadn't happened yet.

And then all four photos had come true.

Greg felt a chill as the lift doors opened and the small crowd of people moved forwards to squeeze inside.

What was the truth about the camera? he wondered.

Does the camera *show* the future?

Or does it actually *cause* bad things to happen?

Greg and his friends think it's pretty cool when they find an old camera in a derelict house, *and* it works. But the camera takes *weird* photos, and Greg starts to realize that it's no ordinary camera, and it's creepy – more than that, it's *evil*.

Goosebumps

SAY CHEESE AND DIE!

R.L. STINE

Hippo

Scholastic Children's Books,
Commonwealth House, 1 – 19 New Oxford Street, London WC1A 1NU, UK
a division of Scholastic Ltd
London ~ New York ~ Toronto ~ Sydney ~ Auckland

First published in the USA by Scholastic Inc., 1992
First phblished in the UK by Scholastic Ltd, 1993
Copyright © Parachute Press, Inc., 1992
GOOSEBUMPS is a trademark of Parachute Press, Inc.

ISBN 0 590 55442 5

Printed by Cox & Wyman Ltd, Reading, Berks

20 19 18

"There's nothing to do in Pitts Landing," Michael Warner said, his hands shoved into the pockets of his faded denim cut-offs.

"Yeah. Pitts Landing is the pits," Greg Banks said.

Doug Arthur and Shari Walker muttered their agreement.

Pitts Landing is the Pits. That was the town slogan, according to Greg and his three friends. Actually, Pitts Landing wasn't very different from a lot of small towns with quiet streets of shady lawns and comfortable, old houses.

But here it was, a balmy autumn afternoon, and the four friends were hanging round Greg's drive, kicking at the gravel, wondering what to do for fun and excitement.

"Let's go to Grover's and see if the new comics have come in," Doug suggested.

"We haven't got any money, Bird," Greg told him.

1

Everyone called Doug "Bird" because he looked a lot like a bird. A better nickname might have been "Stork". He had long, skinny legs and took long, stork-like steps. Under his thick tuft of brown hair, which he seldom brushed, he had small, bird-like brown eyes and a long nose that curved like a beak. Doug didn't really like being called Bird, but he was used to it.

"We can still *look* at the comics," Bird insisted.

"Until Grover starts shouting at you," Shari said. She puffed out her cheeks and did a pretty good imitation of the gruff store owner: "*Are you paying or staying?*"

"He thinks he's cool," Greg said, laughing at her imitation. "He's such a jerk."

"I think the new *X-Force* is coming in this week," Bird said.

"You should join the X-Force," Greg said, giving his pal a playful shove. "You could be Bird Man. You'd be great!"

"We should *all* join the X-Force," Michael said. "If we were super-heroes, maybe we'd have something to do."

"No, we wouldn't," Shari quickly replied. "There's no crime to fight in Pitts Landing."

"We could fight crabgrass," Bird suggested. He was the joker in the group.

The others laughed. The four of them had been friends for a long time. Greg and Shari lived next door to each other, and their parents were best

2

friends. Bird and Michael lived round the corner.

"How about a baseball game?" Michael suggested. "We could go down to the playground."

"No way," Shari said. "You can't play with only four people." She pushed back a strand of her crimped, black hair that had fallen over her face. Shari was wearing an oversized yellow sweatshirt over bright green leggings.

"Maybe we'll find some other kids there," Michael said, picking up a handful of gravel from the drive and letting it sift through his chubby fingers. Michael had short red hair, blue eyes, and a face full of freckles. He wasn't exactly fat, but no one could ever call him skinny.

"Come on, let's play baseball," Bird urged. "I need the practice. My Little League starts in a couple of days."

"Little League? In the autumn?" Shari asked.

"It's a new autumn league. The first game is on Tuesday after school," Bird explained.

"Hey—we'll come and watch you," Greg said.

"We'll come and watch you strike out," Shari added. She loved teasing Bird.

"What position are you playing?" Greg asked.

"Backstop," Michael cracked.

No one laughed. Michael's jokes always fell flat.

Bird shrugged. "Probably fielding. How

3

come *you're* not playing, Greg?"

With his big shoulders and muscular arms and legs, Greg was the natural athlete of the group. He was blond and good-looking, with flashing grey-green eyes and a wide, friendly smile.

"My brother Terry was supposed to go and sign me up, but he forgot," Greg said, making a disgusted face.

"Where *is* Terry?" Shari asked. She had a tiny crush on Greg's older brother.

"He's got a job on Saturdays and after school. At the Dairy Freeze," Greg told her.

"Let's go to the Dairy Freeze!" Michael exclaimed enthusiastically.

"We haven't got any money—remember?" Bird said glumly.

"Terry'll give us free cones," Michael said, turning a hopeful gaze on Greg.

"Yeah. Free cones. But no ice cream in them," Greg told him. "You know what a square my brother is."

"This is boring," Shari complained, watching a robin hop across the pavement. "It's boring standing around talking about how bored we are."

"We could *sit down* and talk about how bored we are," Bird suggested, twisting his mouth into the goofy half-smile he always wore when he was making a stupid joke.

4

"Let's go for a walk or a jog or something," Shari insisted. She made her way across the lawn and began walking, balancing her white high-tops on the edge of the kerb, waving her arms like a tightrope walker.

The boys followed, imitating her in an impromptu game of Follow the Leader, all of them balancing on the kerb edge as they walked.

A curious cocker spaniel came bursting out of the neighbours' hedge, yapping excitedly. Shari stopped to pet him. The dog, its stub of a tail wagging furiously, licked her hand a few times. Then the dog lost interest and disappeared back into the hedge.

The four friends continued down the road, playfully trying to knock each other off the kerb as they walked. They crossed the street and continued on past the school. A couple of boys were shooting baskets, and some little kids playing football on the practice baseball pitch, but no one they knew.

The road curved away from the school. They followed it past familiar houses. Then, just beyond a small wooded area, they stopped and looked up a sloping lawn, the grass uncut for weeks, tall weeds poking out everywhere, the shrubs ragged and overgrown.

At the top of the lawn, nearly hidden in the shadows of enormous, old oak trees, sprawled a large, ramshackle house. The house, anyone could see, had once been grand. It was grey shingle, three stories tall, with a wraparound screened porch, a sloping red roof, and tall chimneys on either end. But the broken windows on the first floor, the cracked, weather-stained shingles, the bare spots on the roof, and the shutters hanging loosely beside the dust-smeared windows were evidence of the house's neglect.

Everyone in Pitts Landing knew it as the Coffman house. Coffman was the name painted on the postbox that tilted on its broken pole over the front path.

But the house had been deserted for years—ever since Greg and his friends could remember.

And people liked to tell weird stories about the house: ghost stories and wild tales about murders and ghastly things that happened there. Most likely, none of them were true.

"Hey—I know what we can do for excitement," Michael said, staring up at the house bathed in shadows.

"Huh? What are you talking about?" Greg asked warily.

"Let's go into the Coffman house," Michael said, starting to make his way across the weed-choked lawn.

"Whoa. Are you crazy?" Greg called, hurrying to catch up with him.

"Let's go in," Michael said, his blue eyes

catching the light of the late afternoon sun filtering down through the tall oak trees. "We wanted an adventure. Something a little exciting, right? Come on—let's check it out."

Greg hesitated and stared up at the house. A cold chill ran down his back.

Before he could reply, a dark form leapt up from the shadows of the tall weeds and attacked him!

Greg toppled backwards onto the ground. "Aah!" he screamed. Then he realized the others were laughing.

"It's that stupid cocker spaniel!" Shari cried. "He followed us!"

"Go home, dog. Go home!" Bird shooed the dog away.

The dog trotted to the kerb, turned round, and stared back at them, its stubby tail wagging furiously.

Feeling embarrassed that he'd become so frightened, Greg slowly pulled himself to his feet, expecting his friends to give him grief. But they were staring up at the Coffman house thoughtfully.

"Yeah, Michael's right," Bird said, slapping Michael hard on the back, so hard Michael winced and turned to push Bird. "Let's see what it's like in there."

"No way," Greg said, hanging back. "I mean,

the place is pretty creepy, don't you think?"

"So?" Shari challenged him, joining Michael and Bird, who repeated her question: "So?"

"So . . . I don't know," Greg replied. He didn't like being the sensible one of the group. Everyone always made fun of the sensible one. He'd rather be the wild and wacky one. But, somehow, he always ended up sensible.

"I don't think we should go in there," he said, staring up at the neglected old house.

"Are you chicken?" Bird asked.

"Chicken!" Michael joined in.

Bird began to cluck loudly, tucking his hands into his armpits and flapping his arms. With his beady eyes and beaky nose, he looked just like a chicken.

Greg didn't want to laugh, but he couldn't help it.

Bird *always* made him laugh.

The clucking and flapping seemed to end the discussion. They were standing at the foot of the broken concrete steps that led up to the screened porch.

"Look. The window next to the front door is broken," Shari said. "We can just reach in and open the door."

"This is cool," Michael said enthusiastically.

"Are we really doing this?" Greg, being the sensible one, had to ask. "I mean—what about Spidey?"

Spidey was a weird-looking man of about fifty or sixty they'd all seen lurking about town. He dressed entirely in black and crept along on long, slender legs. He looked just like a black spider, so the kids all called him Spidey.

Most likely he was a homeless person. No one really knew anything about him—where he'd come from, where he lived. But a lot of kids had seen him hanging round the Coffman house.

"Maybe Spidey doesn't like visitors," Greg warned.

But Shari was already reaching in through the broken windowpane to unlock the front door. And after little effort, she turned the brass knob and the heavy wooden door swung open.

One by one, they walked through the front entrance, Greg reluctantly bringing up the rear. It was dark inside the house. Only narrow beams of sunlight managed to trickle down through the heavy trees in front, creating pale circles of light on the worn brown carpet at their feet.

The floorboards squeaked as Greg and his friends made their way past the living room, which was bare except for a couple of overturned grocery shop boxes against one wall.

Spidey's furniture? Greg wondered.

The living room carpet, as threadbare as the one by the front door, had a dark oval stain in the centre of it. Greg and Bird, stopping in the doorway, both noticed it at the same time.

"Think it's blood?" Bird asked, his tiny eyes lighting up with excitement.

Greg felt a chill on the back of his neck. "Probably ketchup," he replied. Bird laughed and slapped him hard on the back.

Shari and Michael were exploring the kitchen. They were staring at the dust-covered kitchen worktop as Greg came up behind them. He saw immediately what had captured their attention. Two fat, grey mice were standing on the work-top, staring back at them.

"They're cute," Shari said. "They look just like cartoon mice."

The sound of her voice made the two rodents scamper along the worktop, round the sink, and out of sight.

"They're gross," Michael said, making a disgusted face. "I think they were rats—not mice."

"Rats have long tails. Mice don't," Greg told him.

"They were definitely rats," Bird muttered, pushing past them and out into the hall. He disappeared towards the front of the house.

Shari reached up and pulled open a cupboard unit over the worktop. Empty. "I suppose Spidey never uses the kitchen," she said.

"Well, I didn't *think* he was a gourmet chef," Greg joked.

He followed her into the long, narrow dining

11

room, as bare and dusty as the other rooms. A low chandelier still hung from the ceiling, so brown with caked dust, it was impossible to tell that it was glass.

"Looks like a haunted house," Greg said softly.

"Boo," Shari replied.

"There's not much to see in here," Greg complained, following her back to the dark hallway. "Unless you get a thrill from cobwebs."

Suddenly, a loud *crack* made him jump.

Shari laughed and squeezed his shoulder.

"What was *that*?" he cried, unable to stifle his fear.

"Old houses *do* things like that," she said. "They make noises for no reason at all."

"I think we should leave," Greg insisted, embarrassed again that he'd acted so frightened. "I mean, it's boring in here."

"It's sort of exciting being somewhere we're not supposed to be," Shari said, peering into a dark, empty room—probably a study or something at one time.

"I suppose so," Greg replied uncertainly.

They bumped into Michael. "Where's Bird?" Greg asked.

"I think he went down to the basement," Michael replied.

"Huh? The basement?"

Michael pointed to an open door at the right,

off the hall. "The stairs are there."

The three of them made their way to the top of the stairs. They peered down into the darkness. "Bird?"

From somewhere deep in the basement, his voice floated up to them in a horrified scream: "Help! It's got me! Somebody—please help! It's *got* me!"

"It's got me! It's got me!"

At the sound of Bird's terrified cries, Greg pushed past Shari and Michael, who stood frozen in open-mouthed horror. Practically flying down the steep staircase, Greg called out to his friend, "I'm coming, Bird! What *is it*?"

His heart pounding, Greg stopped at the bottom of the stairs, every muscle tight with fear. His eyes searched frantically through the smoky light pouring in from the basement windows up near the ceiling.

"Bird?"

There he was, sitting comfortably, calmly, on an overturned metal dustbin, his legs crossed, a broad smile on his birdlike face. "Gotcha," he said softly, and burst out laughing.

"What *is* it? What *happened*?" came the frightened voices of Shari and Michael. They clamoured down the stairs, coming to a stop beside Greg.

It took them only a few seconds to realize the situation.

"Another stupid joke?" Michael asked, his voice still trembling with fear.

"Bird—you were winding us up again?" Shari sighed, shaking her head.

Enjoying his moment, Bird nodded, with his peculiar half-grin. "You lot are too easy," he scoffed.

"But, Doug—" Shari started. She only called him Doug when she was upset with him. "Haven't you ever heard of the boy who cried wolf? What if something really bad happens one day, and you really need help, and we think you're just kidding?"

"What could happen?" Bird replied smugly. He stood up and gestured around the basement. "Look—it's brighter down here than upstairs."

He was right. Sunlight from the back garden cascaded down through four long windows at ground level, near the ceiling of the basement.

"I still think we should get out of here," Greg insisted, his eyes moving quickly round the large, cluttered room.

Behind Bird's overturned dustbin stood a makeshift table made out of a sheet of plywood resting on four paint cans. A nearly flat mattress, dirty and stained, rested against the wall, a faded wool blanket folded at the foot.

15

"Spidey must *live* down here!" Michael exclaimed.

Bird kicked his way through a pile of empty food boxes that had been tossed all over the floor—TV dinners, mostly. "Hey, a Hungry Man dinner!' he exclaimed. "Where does Spidey heat these up?"

"Maybe he eats them frozen," Shari suggested. "You know. Like ice pops."

She made her way towards a towering oak wardrobe and pulled open the doors. "Wow! This is *excellent*!" she declared. "Look!" She pulled out a ratty-looking fur coat and wrapped it round her shoulders. "Excellent!" she repeated, twirling in the old coat.

From across the room, Greg could see that the wardrobe was stuffed with old clothing. Michael and Bird hurried to join Shari and began pulling out strange-looking pairs of bell-bottom trousers, yellowed dress shirts with pleats down the front, tie-dyed neckties that were about a foot wide, and brightly-coloured scarves and bandannas.

"Hey, you lot—" Greg warned. "Don't you think maybe those belong to somebody?"

Bird spun round, a fuzzy red boa wrapped around his neck and shoulders. "Yeah. These are Spidey's dressing-up clothes," he cracked.

"How about this *baad* hat?" Shari said, turning round to show off the bright purple, wide-brimmed hat she had pulled on.

"Great," Michael said, examining a long blue cape. "This stuff must be at least twenty-five years old. It's awesome. How could someone just leave it here?"

"Maybe they're coming back for it," Greg suggested.

As his friends explored the contents of the wardrobe, Greg wandered to the other end of the basement. A large boiler occupied the far wall, its ducts covered in thick cobwebs. Partially hidden by the boiler ducts, Greg could see stairs, probably leading to an outside exit.

Wooden shelves lined the adjoining wall, cluttered with old paint cans, rags, newspapers, and rusty tools.

Whoever lived here must have been a real handyman, Greg thought, examining a wooden worktable in front of the shelves. A metal vice was clamped to the edge of the worktable. Greg turned the handle, expecting the jaws of the vice to open.

But to his surprise, as he turned the vice handle, a door just above the worktable popped open. Greg pulled the door all the way open, revealing a hidden cabinet shelf.

Resting on the shelf was a camera.

17

For a long moment, Greg just stared at the camera.

Something told him the camera was hidden away for a reason.

Something told him he shouldn't touch it. He should close the secret door and walk away.

But he couldn't resist it.

He reached onto the hidden shelf and took the camera in his hands.

It pulled out easily. Then, to Greg's surprise, the door instantly snapped shut with a loud *bang*.

Weird, he thought, turning the camera in his hands.

What a strange place to leave a camera. Why would someone put it here? If it were valuable enough to hide in a secret cabinet, why didn't they take it with them?

Greg eagerly examined the camera. It was large and surprisingly heavy, with a long lens.

Perhaps a telephoto lens, he thought.

Greg was very interested in cameras. He had a cheap automatic camera, which took okay photos. But he was saving his pocket money in the hopes of buying a really good camera with a lot of lenses.

He loved looking at camera magazines, studying the different models, picking out the ones he wanted to buy.

Sometimes he daydreamed about travelling around the world, going to amazing places, mountaintops and hidden jungle rivers. He'd take photos of everything he saw and become a famous photographer.

His camera at home was just too crummy. That's why all his pictures came out too dark or too light, and everyone in them had glowing red dots in their eyes.

Greg wondered if this camera were any good.

Raising the viewfinder to his eye, he sighted around the room. He came to a stop on Michael, who was wearing two bright yellow feather boas and a white Stetson hat and had climbed to the top of the steps to pose.

"Wait! Hold it!" Greg cried, moving closer, raising the camera to his eye. "Let me take your picture, Michael."

"Where'd you find that?" Bird asked.

"Does that thing have film in it?" Michael demanded.

19

"I don't know," Greg said. "Let's see."

Leaning against the railing, Michael struck what he considered a sophisticated pose.

Greg pointed the camera up and focused carefully. It took a short while for his finger to locate the shutter button. "Okay, ready? Say cheese."

"Cheddar," Michael said, grinning down at Greg as he held his pose against the railing.

"Very funny. Michael's a riot," Bird said sarcastically.

Greg centred Michael in the viewfinder frame, then pressed the shutter button.

The camera clicked and flashed.

Then it made an electronic whirring sound. A slot pulled open on the bottom, and a cardboard square slid out.

"Hey—it's one of those automatic-developing cameras," Greg exclaimed. He pulled the square of cardboard out and examined it. "Look—the picture is starting to develop."

"Let me see," Michael called down, leaning on the railing.

But before he could start down the stairs, everyone heard a loud crunching sound.

They all looked up to the source of the sound—and saw the banister break away and Michael go sailing over the edge.

"Noooooo!" Michael screamed as he toppled to the floor, arms outstretched, the feather boas flying behind him like animal tails.

20

He turned in the air, then hit the concrete hard on his back, his eyes frozen wide in astonishment and fright.

He bounced once.

Then cried out again: "My ankle! Owwww! My ankle!" He grabbed at the injured ankle, then quickly let go with a loud gasp. It hurt too much to touch it.

"*Ohhh*—my ankle!"

Still holding the camera and the photo, Greg rushed to Michael. Shari and Bird did the same.

"We'll go and get help," Shari told Michael, who was still on his back, groaning in pain.

But then they heard the ceiling creak.

Footsteps. Above them.

Someone was in the house.

Someone was approaching the basement stairs.

They were going to be caught.

The footsteps above grew louder.

The four friends exchanged frightened glances. "We've got to get *out* of here," Shari whispered.

The ceiling creaked.

"You can't leave me here!" Michael protested. He pulled himself into a sitting position.

"Quick—stand up," Bird instructed.

Michael struggled to his feet. "I can't stand on this foot." His face revealed his panic.

"We'll help you," Shari said, turning her eyes to Bird. "I'll take one arm. You take the other."

Bird obediently moved forward and pulled Michael's arm around his shoulder.

"Okay, let's move!" Shari whispered, supporting Michael from the other side.

"But how do we get out?" Bird asked breathlessly.

The footsteps grew louder. The ceiling creaked under their weight.

"We can't go up the stairs," Michael whispered, leaning on Shari and Bird.

"There's another staircase behind the boiler," Greg told them, pointing.

"It leads out?" Michael asked, wincing from his ankle pain.

"Probably."

Greg led the way. "Just pray the door isn't padlocked or something."

"We're praying. We're praying!" Bird declared.

"We're outta here!" Shari said, groaning under the weight of Michael's arm.

Leaning heavily against Shari and Bird, Michael hobbled after Greg, and they made their way to the stairs behind the boiler. The stairs, they saw, led to wooden double doors up on ground level.

"I don't see a padlock," Greg said warily. "Please, doors—be open!"

"*Hey—who's down there*?" an angry man's voice called from behind them.

"It's—it's Spidey!" Michael stammered.

"Hurry!" Shari urged, giving Greg a frightened push. "Come *on*!"

Greg put the camera down on the top step. Then he reached up and grabbed the handles of the double doors.

"*Who's down there*?"

Spidey sounded closer, angrier.

"The doors could be locked from the outside," Greg whispered, hesitating.

"Just *push* them, man!" Bird pleaded.

Greg took a deep breath and pushed with all his strength.

The doors didn't budge.

"We're trapped," he told them.

"Now what?" Michael whined.

"Try again," Bird urged Greg. "Maybe they're just stuck." He slid out from under Michael's arm. "Here. I'll help you."

Greg moved over to give Bird room to come up beside him. "Ready?" he asked. "One, two, three—*push*!"

Both boys pushed against the heavy wooden doors with all their might.

And the doors swung open.

"Okay! *Now* we're outta here!" Shari declared happily.

Picking up the camera, Greg led the way out. The back garden, he saw, was as weed-choked and overgrown as the front. An enormous limb had fallen off an old oak tree, probably during a storm, and was lying half in the tree, half on the ground.

Somehow, Bird and Shari managed to drag Michael up the steps and onto the grass. "Can you walk? Try it," Bird said.

Still leaning against the two of them, Michael reluctantly pushed his foot down on the ground. He lifted it. Then pushed it again. "Hey, it feels a bit better," he said, surprised.

"Then let's go," Bird said.

They ran to the overgrown hedge that edged along the side of the garden, Michael on his own now, stepping gingerly on the bad ankle, doing his best to keep up. Then, staying in the shadow of the hedge, they made their way round the house to the front.

"All *right*!" Bird cried happily as they reached the street. "We made it!"

Gasping for breath, Greg stopped at the kerb and turned back towards the house. "Look!" he cried, pointing up to the living room window.

A dark figure stood in the window, hands pressed against the glass.

"It's Spidey," Shari said.

"He's just—staring at us," Michael cried.

"Weird," Greg said. "Let's go."

They didn't stop till they got to Michael's house, a sprawling ranch-style house behind a shady front lawn.

"How's the ankle?" Greg asked.

"It's loosened up a lot. It doesn't even hurt that much," Michael said.

"Man, you could've been *killed*!" Bird declared,

wiping sweat off his forehead with the sleeve of his T-shirt.

"Thanks for reminding me," Michael said drily.

"Lucky thing you've got all that extra padding," Bird teased.

"Shut up," Michael muttered.

"Well, you boys wanted adventure," Shari said, leaning back against the trunk of a tree.

"That bloke Spidey is definitely weird," Bird said, shaking his head.

"Did you see the way he was staring at us?" Michael asked. "All dressed in black and everything? He looked like some kind of zombie or something."

"He saw us," Greg said softly, suddenly feeling a chill of dread. "He saw us very clearly. We'd better stay away from there."

"What for?" Michael demanded. "It isn't his house. He's just sleeping there. We could get the police on him."

"But if he's really loony or something, there's no telling what he might do," Greg replied thoughtfully.

"Aw, he's not going to do anything," Shari said quietly. "Spidey doesn't want trouble. He just wants to be left alone."

"Yeah," Michael agreed quickly. "He didn't want us messing around with his stuff. That's why he shouted like that and came after us."

Michael was leaning over, rubbing his ankle. "Hey, where's my picture?" he demanded, straightening up and turning to Greg.

"Huh?"

"You know. The picture you took. With the camera."

"Oh. Right." Greg suddenly realized he still had the camera gripped tightly in his hand. He put it down carefully on the grass and reached into his back pocket. "I put it here when we started to run," he explained.

"Well? Did it come out?" Michael demanded.

The three of them huddled round Greg to get a view of the photo.

"Whoa—hold on a minute!" Greg cried, staring hard at the small, square photo. "Something's wrong. What's going *on* here?"

The four friends gaped at the photograph in Greg's hand, their mouths dropping open in surprise.

The camera had caught Michael in midair as he fell through the broken railing to the floor.

"That's impossible!" Shari cried.

"You took the picture *before* I fell!" Michael declared, grabbing the photo out of Greg's hand so that he could study it close up. "I remember it."

"You remembered wrong," Bird said, moving to get another look at it over Michael's shoulder. "You were falling, man. What a great action shot." He picked up the camera. "This is a good camera you stole, Greg."

"I didn't steal it"—Greg started—"I mean, I didn't realize—"

"I *wasn't* falling!" Michael insisted, tilting the picture in his hand, studying it from every angle. "I was posing, remember? I had a big, goofy smile on my face, and I was posing."

"I remember the goofy smile," Bird said, handing the camera back to Greg. "Do you have any *other* expression?"

"You're not funny, Bird," Michael muttered. He pocketed the picture.

"Weird," Greg said. He glanced at his watch. "Hey—I've got to get going."

He said goodbye to the others and headed for home. The afternoon sun was lowering behind a cluster of palm trees, casting long, shifting shadows over the pavement.

He had promised his mother he'd straighten up his room and help with the vacuuming before dinner. And now he was late.

What was that strange car in the drive? he wondered, jogging across the neighbour's lawn towards his house.

It was a navy-blue Taurus estate car. Brand new.

Dad's picked up our new car! he realized.

Wow! Greg stopped to admire it. It still had the sticker glued to the door window. He pulled open the driver's door, leaned in, and smelled the vinyl upholstery.

Mmmmmmm. That new-car smell.

He inhaled deeply again. It smelled so good. So fresh and new.

He closed the door hard, appreciating the solid *clunk* it made as it closed.

What a great new car, he thought excitedly.

He raised the camera to his eye and took a few steps back off the drive.

I've *got* to take a picture of this, he thought. To remember what the car was like when it was totally new.

He backed up until he had framed the entire profile of the car in the viewfinder. Then he pressed the shutter button.

As before, the camera clicked loudly, the flash flashed, and with an electronic *whirr*, a square undeveloped photo of grey and yellow slid out of the bottom.

Carrying the camera and the snapshot, Greg ran into the house through the front door. "I'm home!" he called. "Down in a minute!" And hurried up the carpeted stairs to his room.

"Greg? Is that you? Your father's home," his mother called from downstairs.

"I know. Be right down. Sorry I'm late!" Greg shouted back.

I'd better hide the camera, he decided. If Mum or Dad see it, they'll want to know whose it is and where I got it. And I won't be able to answer those questions.

"Greg—did you see the new car? Are you coming down?" his mother called impatiently from the bottom of the stairs.

"I'm coming!" he yelled.

His eyes searched frantically for a good hiding place.

Under his bed?

No. His mum might vacuum under there and discover it.

Then Greg remembered the secret compartment in his headboard. He had discovered the compartment years ago when his parents had bought him a new bedroom set. Quickly, he shoved the camera in.

Peering into the mirror above his chest of drawers, he gave his blond hair a quick brush, rubbed a black soot smudge off his cheek with one hand, then started for the door.

He stopped at the doorway.

The snapshot of the car. Where had he put it?

It took a few seconds to remember that he had tossed it onto his bed. Curious about how it had come out, he turned back to retrieve it.

"Oh, no!"

He uttered a low cry as he gazed at the photograph.

What's going on here? Greg wondered.

He brought the photo up close to his face.

This isn't right, he thought. How can this *be*?

The blue Taurus estate car in the photo was a mess. It looked as if it had been in a terrible accident. The windscreen was shattered. Metal was twisted and bent. The door on the driver's side had caved in.

The car appeared *wrecked*!

"This is impossible!" Greg uttered aloud.

"Greg, where *are* you?" his mother called. "We're all hungry, and you're keeping us waiting."

"Sorry," he answered, unable to take his eyes off the photo. "Coming."

He shoved it into the top drawer of his chest of drawers and made his way downstairs. The image of the wrecked car burned in his mind.

Just to make sure, he crossed the living room and peeped out of the front window at the drive.

33

There stood the new car, sparkling in the glow of the setting sun. Shiny and perfect.

He turned and walked into the dining room where his brother and his parents were already sitting. "The new car is awesome, Dad," Greg said, trying to shake the photo's image from his thoughts.

But he kept seeing the twisted metal, the caved-in driver's door, the shattered windscreen.

"After dinner," Greg's dad announced happily, "I'm taking you all for a drive in the new car!"

"Mmmm. This is great chicken, Mum," Greg's brother Terry said, chewing as he talked.

"Thanks for the compliment," Mrs Banks said drily, "but it's veal—not chicken."

Greg and his dad burst out laughing. Terry's face grew bright red. "Well," he said, still chewing, "it's such excellent veal, it tastes as good as chicken!"

"I don't know why I bother to cook," Mrs Banks sighed.

Mr Banks changed the subject. "How are things at the Dairy Freeze?" he asked.

"We ran out of vanilla this afternoon," Terry said, forking a small potato and shoving it whole into his mouth. He chewed it briefly, then gulped it down. "People were annoyed about that."

"I don't think I can go for the car ride," Greg said, staring down at his dinner, which he'd hardly touched. "I mean—"

"Why not?" his father asked.

"Well . . ." Greg searched his mind for a good reason. He needed to make one up, but his mind was a blank.

He couldn't tell them the truth.

That he had taken a photograph of Michael, and it showed Michael falling. Then a few seconds later, Michael had fallen.

And now he had taken one of the new car. And the car was wrecked in the photo.

Greg didn't really know what it meant. But he was suddenly filled with this powerful feeling, of dread, of fear, of . . . he didn't know what.

A kind of troubled feeling he'd never had before.

But he couldn't tell them any of that. It was too weird. Too *crazy*.

"I . . . made plans to go over to Michael's," he lied, staring down at his plate.

"Well, phone him and tell him you'll see him tomorrow," Mr Banks said, slicing his veal. "That's no problem."

"Well, I'm kind of not feeling very well, either," Greg said.

"What's wrong?" Mrs Banks asked with instant concern. "Have you got a temperature? I thought you looked a little flushed when you came in."

"No," Greg replied uncomfortably. "No temperature. I just feel tired, not very hungry."

"Can I have your chicken—I mean, veal?" Terry asked eagerly. He reached for his fork across the table and nabbed the cutlet off Greg's plate.

"Well, a nice drive might make you feel better," Greg's dad said, eyeing Greg suspiciously. "You know, some fresh air. You can stretch out in the back if you want."

"But, Dad—" Greg stopped. He had used up all the excuses he could think of. They would *never* believe him if he said he needed to stay at home and do homework on a Saturday night!

"You're coming with us, and that's final," Mr Banks said, still studying Greg closely. "You've been dying for this new car to arrive. I really don't understand your problem."

Neither do I, Greg admitted to himself.

I don't understand it at all. Why am I so afraid of going in the new car? Just because there's something wrong with that stupid camera?

I'm being silly, Greg thought, trying to shake away the feeling of dread that had taken away his appetite.

"Okay, Dad. Great," he said, forcing a smile. "I'll come."

"Are there any more potatoes?" Terry asked.

"It's so easy to drive," Mr Banks said, as he accelerated onto the street. "It handles like a small car, not like an estate car."

"Plenty of room back here, Dad," Terry said, scooting low in the back seat beside Greg, raising his knees to the back of the front seat.

"Hey, look—there's a drinks holder that pulls out from the dashboard!" Greg's mother exclaimed. "That's handy."

"Awesome, Mum," Terry said sarcastically.

"Well, we've never had a drinks holder before," Mrs Banks replied. She turned back to the two boys. "Are your seat belts buckled? Do they work properly?"

"Yeah. They're okay," Terry replied.

"They checked them at the showroom, before I took the car," Mr Banks said, signalling to move into the left lane.

A truck roared by, spitting a cloud of exhaust behind it. Greg stared out of the front window.

His door window was still covered by the new car sticker.

Mr Banks pulled off the road, onto a nearly empty four-lane motorway that curved towards the west. The setting sun was a red ball low on the horizon in a charcoal-grey sky.

"Put the pedal to the metal, Dad," Terry urged, sitting up and leaning forward. "Let's see what this car can do."

Mr Banks obediently pressed his foot on the accelerator. "The cruising speed seems to be about sixty," he said.

"Slow down," Mrs Banks scolded. "You know the speed limit is fifty-five."

"I'm just testing it," Greg's dad said defensively. "You know. Making sure the transmission doesn't slip or anything."

Greg stared at the glowing speedometer. They were doing seventy now.

"Slow down. I mean it," Mrs Banks insisted. "You're acting like a crazy teenager."

"That's me!" Mr Banks replied, laughing. "This is *awesome*!" he said, imitating Terry, ignoring his wife's pleas to slow down.

They roared past a couple of small cars in the right lane. Headlights of cars moving towards them were a bright white blur in the darkening night.

"Hey, Greg, you've been awfully quiet," his mother said. "You feeling okay?"

"Yeah. I'm okay," Greg said softly.

He wished his dad would slow down. He was doing seventy-five now.

"What do you think, Greg?" Mr Banks asked, steering with his left hand as his right hand searched the dashboard. "Where's the light switch? I should turn on my headlights."

"The car's great," Greg replied, trying to sound enthusiastic. But he couldn't shake away the fear, couldn't get the photo of the mangled car out of his mind.

"Where's that stupid light switch? It's got to be here somewhere," Mr Banks said.

As he glanced down at the unfamiliar dashboard, the car swerved to the left.

"Dad—look out for that truck!" Greg screamed.

Horns blared.

A powerful blast of air swept over the estate car, like a giant ocean wave pushing it to the side.

Mr Banks swerved the estate car to the right. The truck rumbled past.

"Sorry," Greg's dad said, eyes straight ahead, slowing the car to sixty, fifty-five, fifty . . .

"I *told* you to slow down," Mrs Banks scolded, shaking her head. "We could've been killed!"

"I was trying to find the lights," he explained. "Oh. Here thcy are. On the steering wheel." He clicked on the headlights.

"You boys okay?" Mrs Banks asked, turning to check on them.

"Yeah. Fine," Terry said, sounding a little shaken. The truck would have hit his side of the car.

"I'm okay," Greg said. "Can we go back now?"

"Don't you want to keep going?" Mr Banks asked, unable to hide his disappointment. "I thought we'd keep going to Santa Clara. Stop and get some ice cream or something."

"Greg's right," Mrs Banks said softly to her husband. "Enough for tonight, dear. Let's turn round."

"The truck didn't come *that* close," Mr Banks argued. But he obediently turned off the motorway and they headed for home.

Later, safe and sound up in his room, Greg took the photograph out of the drawer and examined it. There was the new car, the driver's side caved in, the windscreen shattered.

"Weird," he said aloud, and placed the photo in the secret compartment in his headboard where he had stashed the camera. "Definitely weird."

He pulled the camera out of its hiding place and turned it around in his hands.

I'll try it once more, he decided.

He walked to his chest of drawers and aimed at the mirror above it.

I'll take a picture of myself in the mirror, he thought.

He raised the camera, then changed his mind. That won't work, he realized. The flash will reflect back and spoil the photo.

Gripping the camera in one hand, he made his way across the landing to Terry's room. His brother was at his desk, typing away on his computer keyboard, his face bathed in the blue light of the monitor screen.

"Terry, can I take your photo?" Greg asked meekly, holding up the camera.

Terry typed some more, then looked up from the screen. "Hey—where'd you get the camera?"

"Uh . . . Shari lent it to me," Greg told him, thinking quickly. Greg didn't like lying. But he didn't feel like explaining to Terry how he and his friends had sneaked into the Coffman house and he had made off with the camera.

"So can I take your picture?" Greg asked.

"I'll probably break your camera," Terry joked.

"I think it's already broken," Greg told him. "That's why I want to test it on you."

"Go ahead," Terry said. He stuck out his tongue and crossed his eyes.

Greg snapped the shutter. An undeveloped photo slid out of the slot in front.

"Thanks. See you." Greg headed for the door.

"Hey—don't I get to see it?" Terry called after him.

"If it comes out," Greg said, and hurried across the landing to his room.

He sat down on the edge of the bed. Holding the photo in his lap, he stared at it intently as it developed. The yellows filled in first. Then the reds appeared, followed by shades of blue.

43

"Whoa," Greg muttered as his brother's face came into view. "There's something definitely wrong here."

In the photo, Terry's eyes weren't crossed, and his tongue wasn't sticking out. His expression was grim, frightened. He looked very upset.

As the background came into focus, Greg had another surprise. Terry wasn't in his room. He was outdoors. There were trees in the background. And a house.

Greg stared at the house. It looked so familiar.

Was that the house across the street from the playground?

He took one more look at Terry's frightened expression. Then he tucked the photo and the camera into his secret headboard compartment and carefully closed it.

The camera must be broken, he decided, getting changed for bed.

It was the best explanation he could come up with.

Lying in bed, staring up at the shifting shadows on the ceiling, he decided not to think about it any more.

A broken camera wasn't worth worrying about.

On Tuesday afternoon after school, Greg hurried to meet Shari at the playground to watch Bird's Little League game.

It was a warm autumn afternoon, the sun high in a cloudless sky. The outfield grass had been freshly mowed and filled the air with its sharp, sweet smell.

Greg crossed the grass and squinted into the bright sunlight, searching for Shari. Both teams were warming up on the sides of the pitch, yelling and laughing, the sound of balls popping into gloves competing with their loud voices.

A few parents and several kids had come to watch. Some were standing around, some sitting in the low bleachers along the first base line.

Greg spotted Shari behind the backstop and waved to her. "Did you bring the camera?" she asked eagerly, running over to greet him.

He held it up.

"Excellent," she exclaimed, grinning. She reached for it.

"I think it's broken," Greg said, holding on to the camera. "The photos just don't come out right. It's hard to explain."

"Maybe it's not the photos. Maybe it's the photographer," Shari teased.

"Maybe I'll take a photo of you getting a knuckle sandwich," Greg threatened. He raised the camera to his eye and pointed it at her.

"Snap that, and I'll take a picture of you *eating* the camera," Shari threatened playfully. She reached up quickly and pulled the camera from his hand.

"What do you want it for, anyway?" Greg asked, making a half-hearted attempt to grab it back.

Shari held it away from his outstretched hand. "I want to take Bird's picture when he comes to bat. He looks just like an ostrich at the plate."

"I heard that." Bird appeared beside them, pretending to be insulted.

He looked ridiculous in his starched white uniform. The shirt was too big, and the trousers were too short. The cap was the only thing that fitted. It was blue, with a silver dolphin over the peak and the words: PITTS LANDING DOLPHINS.

"What kind of name is 'Dolphins' for a baseball team?" Greg asked, grabbing the peak and turning the cap backwards on Bird's head.

"All the other caps were taken," Bird answered. "We had a choice between the Zephyrs and the Dolphins. None of us knew what Zephyrs were, so we picked Dolphins."

Shari eyed him up and down. "Maybe you lot should play in your ordinary clothes."

"Thanks for the encouragement," Bird replied. He spotted the camera and took it from her. "Hey, you've brought the camera. Has it got any film in it?"

"Yeah. I think so," Greg told him. "Let me see." He reached for the camera, but Bird swung it out of his grasp.

46

"Hey—are you going to share this thing, Greg?" he asked.

"Huh? What do you mean?" Greg reached again for the camera, and again Bird swung it away from him.

"I mean, we all risked our lives down in that basement getting it, right?" Bird said. "We should all share it."

"Well . . ." Greg hadn't thought about it. "I suppose you're right, Bird. But I'm the one who found it. So—"

Shari grabbed the camera out of Bird's hand. "I told Greg to bring it so we could take your photo when you're batting."

"As an example of good form?" Bird asked.

"As a *bad* example," Shari said.

"You lot are just jealous," Bird replied, frowning, "because I'm a natural athlete, and you can't cross the road without falling on your faces." He turned the cap back round to face the front.

"Hey, Bird—get back here!" one of the coaches called from the playing field.

"I've got to go," Bird said, giving them a quick wave and starting to trot back to his teammates.

"No. Wait. Let me take a fast picture now," Greg said.

Bird stopped, turned round, and struck a pose.

"No. I'll take it," Shari insisted.

She started to raise the camera to her eye,

pointing it towards Bird. And as she raised it, Greg grabbed for it.

"Let *me* take it!"

And the camera went off. Clicked and then flashed.

An undeveloped photo slid out.

"Hey, why'd you do that?" Shari asked angrily.

"Sorry," Greg said. "I didn't mean to—"

She pulled the photo out and held it in her hand. Greg and Bird came close to watch it develop.

"What the heck is *that*?" Bird cried, staring hard at the small square as the colours brightened and took shape.

"Oh, wow!" Greg cried.

The photo showed Bird sprawled unconscious on his back on the ground, his mouth twisted open, his neck bent at a frightening angle, his eyes shut tight.

"Hey—what's wrong with this stupid camera?" Bird asked, grabbing the photo out of Shari's hand. He tilted it from side to side, squinting at it. "It's out of focus or something."

"Weird," Greg said, shaking his head.

"*Hey, Bird—get over here!*" the Dolphins' coach called.

"Coming!" Bird handed the picture back to Shari and jogged over to his teammates.

Whistles blew. The two teams stopped their practising and trotted to the benches along the third base line.

"How did this *happen*?" Shari asked Greg, shielding her eyes from the sun with one hand, holding the photo close to her face with the other. "It really looks like Bird is lying on the ground, knocked out or something. But he was standing right in front of us."

"I don't get it. I really don't," Greg replied thoughtfully. "The camera keeps doing that."

Carrying the camera at his side, swinging it by its slender strap, he followed her to a shady spot beside the benches.

"Look how his neck is bent," Shari continued. "It's so *awful.*"

"There's definitely something wrong with the camera," Greg said. He started to tell her about the photo he'd taken of the new car, and the picture of his brother Terry. But she interrupted before he could get the words out.

"—And that picture of Michael. It showed him falling down the stairs before he even fell. It's just so strange."

"I know," Greg agreed.

"Let me see that thing," Shari said and pulled the camera from his hand. "Is there any film left?"

"I can't tell," Greg admitted. "I couldn't find a film roll or anything."

Shari examined the camera closely, rolling it over in her hands. "It doesn't say anywhere. How can you tell if it's loaded or not?"

Greg shrugged.

The baseball game got under way. The Dolphins were the visiting team. The other team, the Cardinals, jogged out to take their positions on the field.

A kid in the benches dropped his lemonade can. It hit the ground and spilled, and the kid started to cry. An old estate car filled with teenagers cruised by, its radio blaring, its horn honking.

"Where do you put the film in?" Shari asked impatiently.

Greg stepped closer to help her examine it. "Here, I think," he said, pointing. "Doesn't the back come off?"

Shari fiddled with it. "No, I don't think so. Most of these automatic-developing cameras load in the front."

She pulled at the back, but the camera wouldn't open. She tried pulling off the bottom. No better luck. Turning the camera, she tried pulling off the lens. It wouldn't budge.

Greg took the camera from her. "There's no slot or opening in the front."

"Well, what kind of camera is it anyway?" Shari demanded.

"Uh . . . let's see." Greg studied the front, examined the top of the lens, then turned the camera over and studied the back.

He stared up at her with a surprised look on his face. "There's no brand name. Nothing."

"How can a camera not have a name?" Shari shouted in exasperation. She snatched the camera away from him and examined it closely, squinting her eyes against the bright afternoon sunshine.

Finally, she handed the camera back to him, defeated. "You're right, Greg. No name. No

51

words of any kind. Nothing. What a stupid camera," she added angrily.

"Whoa. Hold on," Greg told her. "It's not my camera, remember? I didn't buy it. I took it from the Coffman house."

"Well, let's at least work out how to open it up and look inside," Shari said.

The first Dolphin batter popped up to the second baseman. The second batter struck out on three straight swings. The dozen or so spectators shouted encouragement to their team.

The little kid who had dropped his drink continued to cry. Three kids cycled by on bikes, waving to friends on the teams, but not stopping to watch.

"I've tried and tried, but I can't work out how to open it," Greg admitted.

"Give it to me," Shari said and grabbed the camera away from him. "There has to be a button or something. There has to be some way of opening it. This is ridiculous."

When she couldn't find a button or lever of any kind, she tried pulling the back off once again, prising it with her fingernails. Then she tried turning the lens, but it wouldn't turn.

"I'm not giving up," she said, gritting her teeth. "I'm not. This camera has to open. It *has* to!"

"Give up. You're going to wreck it," Greg warned, reaching for it.

"Wreck it? How could I wreck it?" Shari demanded. "It has no moving parts. Nothing!"

"This is impossible," Greg said.

Making a disgusted face, she handed the camera to him. "Okay, I give up. Look it over yourself, Greg."

He took the camera, started to raise it to his face, then stopped.

Uttering a low cry of surprise, his mouth dropped open and his eyes gaped straight ahead. Startled, Shari turned to follow his shocked gaze.

"Oh *no*!"

There on the ground a few metres outside the first base line, lay Bird. He was sprawled on his back, his neck bent at an odd and unnatural angle, his eyes shut tight.

13

"Bird!" Shari cried.

Greg's breath caught in his throat. He felt as if he were choking. "Oh!" he finally managed to cry out in a shrill, raspy voice.

Bird didn't move.

Shari and Greg, running side by side at full speed, reached him together.

"Bird?" Shari knelt down beside him. "Bird?"

Bird opened one eye. "Gotcha," he said quietly. The weird half-smile formed on his face, and he exploded into high-pitched laughter.

It took Shari and Greg a while to react. They both stood open-mouthed, gaping at their laughing friend.

Then, his heart beginning to slow to normal, Greg reached down, grabbed Bird with both hands, and pulled him roughly to his feet.

"I'll hold him while you hit him," Greg offered, holding Bird from behind.

"Hey, wait—" Bird protested, struggling to

squirm out of Greg's grasp.

"Good plan," Shari said, grinning.

"Ow! Hey—let go! Come on! Let go!" Bird protested, trying unsuccessfully to wrestle free. "Come on! What's your problem? It was a joke, okay?"

"Very funny," Shari said, giving Bird a playful punch on the shoulder. "You're hilarious, Bird."

Bird finally freed himself with a hard tug and danced away from both of them. "I just wanted to show you how pathetic it is to get all worked up about that stupid camera."

"But, Bird—" Greg started.

"It's just broken, that's all," Bird said, brushing blades of recently cut grass off his uniform trousers. "You think because it showed Michael falling down those stairs, there's something strange about it. But that's stupid. Really stupid."

"I *know*," Greg replied sharply. "But how do you explain it?"

"I told you, man. It's wrecked. Broken. That's it."

"*Bird—get over here!*" a voice called, and Bird's fielder's glove came flying at his head. He caught it, waved with a grin to Shari and Greg, and jogged to the outfield along with the other members of the Dolphins.

Carrying the camera tightly in one hand, Greg

led the way to the benches. He and Shari sat down on the end of the bottom bench.

Some of the spectators had lost interest in the game already and had left. A few kids had taken a baseball off the field and were having their own game of catch behind the benches. Across the playground, four or five kids were getting a game of football started.

"Bird is such a dork," Greg said, his eyes on the game.

"He scared me to death," Shari exclaimed. "I really thought he was hurt."

"What a clown," Greg muttered.

They watched the game in silence for a while. It wasn't terribly interesting. The Dolphins were losing 12-3 going into the third inning. None of the players were very good.

Greg laughed as a Cardinal batter, a kid from their class named Joe Garden, slugged a ball that sailed out to the field and right over Bird's head.

"That's the third ball that's gone over his head!" Greg cried.

"I suppose he lost it in the sun!" Shari exclaimed, joining in the laughter.

They both watched Bird's long legs storking after the ball. By the time he managed to catch up with it and heave it towards the diamond, Joe Garden had already rounded the bases and scored.

There were loud *boos* from the benches.

The next Cardinal batter stepped up to the plate. A few more kids climbed down from the benches, having seen enough.

"It's so hot here in the sun," Shari said, shielding her eyes with one hand. "And I've got lots of homework. Want to leave?"

"I just want to see the next inning," Greg said, watching the batter swing and miss. "Bird is coming up next inning. I want to stay and *boo* him."

"What are friends for?" Shari said sarcastically.

It took a long while for the Dolphins to get the third out. The Cardinals batted around their entire order.

Greg's T-shirt was drenched with sweat by the time Bird came to the plate in the top of the fourth.

Despite the loud *booing* from Shari and Greg, Bird managed to punch the ball past the shortstop for a single.

"Lucky hit!" Greg yelled, cupping his hands into a megaphone.

Bird pretended not to hear him. He tossed away his batter's helmet, adjusted his cap, and took a short lead off first base.

The next batter swung at the first pitch and fouled it off.

"Let's go," Shari urged, pulling Greg's arm.

"It's too hot. I'm dying of thirst."

"Let's just see if Bird—"

Greg didn't finish his sentence.

The batter hit the next ball hard. It made a loud *thunk* as it left the bat.

A dozen people—players and spectators—cried out as the ball flew across the pitch, a sharp line drive, and slammed into the side of Bird's head with another *thunk*.

Greg watched in horror as the ball bounced off Bird and dribbled away onto the grass. Bird's eyes went wide with disbelief, confusion.

He stood frozen in place on the base path for a long moment.

Then both of his hands shot up above his head, and he uttered a shrill cry, long and loud, like the high-pitched whinny of a horse.

His eyes rolled up in his head. He sank to his knees. Uttered another cry, softer this time. Then collapsed, sprawling onto his back, his neck at an unnatural angle, his eyes closed.

He didn't move.

In seconds, the two coaches and both teams were running out to the fallen player, huddling over him, forming a tight, hushed circle around him.

Crying, "Bird! Bird!" Shari leapt off the benches and began running to the circle of horrified onlookers.

Greg started to follow, but stopped when he saw a familiar figure crossing the road, running and waving to him.

"Terry!" Greg cried.

Why was his brother coming to the playground? Why wasn't he at his after-school job at the Dairy Freeze?

"Terry? What's happening?" Greg cried.

Terry stopped, gasping for breath, sweat pouring down his bright red forehead. "I . . . ran . . . all . . . the . . . way," he managed to utter.

"Terry, what's wrong?" A sick feeling crept up from Greg's stomach.

As Terry approached, his face held the same

frightened expression as in the photograph Greg had snapped of him.

The same frightened expression. With the same house behind him across the street.

The photograph had come true. Just as the one of Bird lying on the ground had come true.

Greg's throat suddenly felt like cotton wool. He realized that his knees were trembling.

"Terry, what *is* it?" he managed to cry.

"It's Dad," Terry said, putting a heavy hand on Greg's shoulder.

"Huh? Dad?"

"You've got to come home, Greg. Dad—he's been in a bad accident."

"An accident?" Greg's head spun. Terry's words weren't making any sense to him.

"In the new car," Terry explained, again placing a heavy hand on Greg's trembling shoulder. "The new car is wrecked. Completely wrecked."

"Oh," Greg gasped, feeling weak.

Terry squeezed his shoulder. "Come on. Hurry."

Holding the camera tightly in one hand, Greg started running after his brother.

Reaching the street, he turned back to the playground to see what was happening with Bird.

A large crowd was still huddled round Bird, blocking him from sight.

But—what was that dark shadow behind the benches? Greg wondered.

Someone—someone all in black—was hiding back there.

Watching Greg?

"Come *on!*" Terry urged.

Greg stared hard at the benches. The dark figure drew back out of sight.

"Come *on*, Greg!"

"I'm coming!" Greg shouted, and followed his brother towards their house.

The hospital walls were pale green. The uniforms worn by the nurses scurrying through the brightly lit corridors were white. The floor tiles beneath Greg's feet as he hurried with his brother towards their father's room were dark brown with orange specks.

Colours.

All Greg could see were blurs of colours, indistinct shapes.

His trainers thudded noisily against the hard tile floor. He could barely hear them over the pounding of his heart.

Wrecked. The car had been wrecked.

Just like in the photo.

Greg and Terry turned a corner. The walls in this corridor were pale yellow. Terry's cheeks were red. Two doctors passed by wearing lime-green surgical gloves.

Colours. Only colours.

Greg blinked, tried to see clearly. But it was all

passing by too fast, all too unreal. Even the sharp hospital smell, that unique aroma of stale food, and disinfectant, couldn't make it real for him.

Then the two brothers entered their father's room, and it all became real.

The colours faded. The images became sharp and clear.

Their mother jumped up from the folding chair beside the bed. "Hi, boys." She clenched a wadded-up tissue in her hand. It was obvious that she had been crying. She forced a tight smile on her face, but her eyes were red-rimmed, her cheeks pale and puffy.

Stopping just inside the doorway of the small room, Greg returned his mother's greeting in a soft, choked voice. Then his eyes, focusing clearly now, turned to his father.

Mr Banks had a mummy-like bandage covering his hair. One arm was in a plastercast. The other lay at his side and had a tube attached just below the wrist, dripping a dark liquid into the arm. The bedsheet was pulled up to his chest.

"Hey—how's it going, boys?" their father asked. His voice sounded muffled, as if coming from far away.

"Dad—" Terry started.

"He's going to be okay," Mrs Banks interrupted, seeing the frightened looks on her sons' faces.

"I feel great," Mr Banks said groggily.

"You don't *look* so great," Greg blurted out, stepping up cautiously to the bed.

"I'm okay. Really," their father insisted. "A few broken bones. That's all." He sighed, then winced from some pain. "I suppose I'm lucky."

"You're very lucky," Mrs Banks agreed quickly.

What's the lucky part? Greg wondered silently to himself. He couldn't take his eyes off the tube stuck into his father's arm.

Again, he thought of the photograph of the car. It was up in his room at home, tucked into the secret compartment in his headboard.

The photo showing the car wreck, the driver's side caved in.

Should he tell them about it?

He couldn't decide.

Would they believe him if he *did* tell them?

"What'd you break, Dad?" Terry asked, sitting down on the radiator in front of the windowsill, shoving his hands into his jeans pockets.

"Your father broke his arm and a few ribs," Mrs Banks answered quickly. "And he had slight concussion. The doctors are checking him for internal injuries. But, so far, so good."

"I was lucky," Mr Banks repeated. He smiled at Greg.

"Dad, I've got to tell you about this photo I took," Greg said suddenly, speaking rigidly, his voice trembling with nervousness. "I took a picture of the new car, and—"

"The car is completely wrecked," Mrs Banks interrupted. Sitting on the edge of the folding chair, she rubbed her fingers, working her wedding ring round and round, something she always did when she was nervous. "I'm glad you boys didn't see it." Her voice caught in her throat. Then she added, "It's a miracle he wasn't more badly hurt."

"This photo—" Greg started again.

"Later," his mother said brusquely. "Okay?" She gave him a meaningful stare.

Greg felt his face grow hot.

This is *important*, he thought.

Then he decided they probably wouldn't believe him, anyway. Who would believe such a crazy story?

"Will we be able to get another new car?" Terry asked.

Mr Banks nodded carefully. "I have to phone the insurance company," he said.

"I'll phone them when I get home," Mrs Banks said. "You don't exactly have a hand free."

Everyone laughed at that, nervous laughter.

"I feel pretty sleepy," Mr Banks said. His eyes were halfway closed, his voice muffled.

"It's the painkillers the doctors gave you," Mrs Banks told him. She leaned forward and patted his hand. "Get some sleep. I'll come back in a few hours."

She stood up, still fiddling with her wedding ring, and motioned with her head towards the door.

"Bye, Dad," Greg and Terry said in unison.

Their father muttered a reply. They followed their mother out of the door.

"What *happened*?" Terry asked as they made their way past a nurses' office, then down the long, pale yellow corridor. "I mean, the accident."

"Some man went straight through a red light," Mrs Banks said, her red-rimmed eyes staring straight ahead. "He ploughed right into your father's side of the car. Said his brakes weren't working." She shook her head, tears forming in the corners of her eyes. "I don't know," she said, sighing. "I just don't know what to say. Thank goodness he's going to be okay."

They turned into the green corridor, walking side by side. Several people were waiting patiently for the lift at the far side of the corridor.

Once again, Greg found himself thinking of the pictures he had taken with the weird camera.

First Michael. Then Terry. Then Bird. Then his father.

All four photos had shown something terrible. Something terrible that hadn't happened yet.

And then all four photos had come true.

Greg felt a chill as the lift doors opened and the small crowd of people moved forwards to squeeze inside.

What was the truth about the camera? he wondered.

Does the camera *show* the future?

Or does it actually *cause* bad things to happen?

"Yeah. I know Bird's okay," Greg said into the phone receiver. "I saw him yesterday, remember? He was lucky. Really lucky. He didn't have concussion or anything."

On the other end of the line—in the house next door—Shari agreed, then repeated her request.

"No, Shari. I really don't want to," Greg replied vehemently.

"*Bring* it," Shari demanded. "It's *my* birthday."

"I don't want to bring the camera. It's not a good idea. Really," Greg told her.

It was the next weekend. Saturday afternoon. Greg had been nearly out of the door, on his way next door to Shari's birthday party, when the phone rang.

"Hi, Greg. Why aren't you on your way to my party?" Shari had asked after he'd run to pick up the phone.

"Because I'm on the phone to you," Greg had replied drily.

"Well, bring the camera, okay?"

Greg hadn't looked at the camera, hadn't removed it from its hiding place since his father's accident.

"I don't want to bring it," he insisted, despite Shari's high-pitched demands. "Don't you understand, Shari? I don't want anyone else to get hurt."

"Oh, Greg," she said, talking to him as if he were a three-year-old. "You don't really believe that, do you? You don't really believe that the camera can hurt people."

Greg was silent for a moment. "I don't know what I believe," he said finally. "I only know that first Michael, then Bird—"

Greg swallowed hard. "And I had a dream, Shari. Last night."

"Huh? What kind of dream?" Shari asked impatiently.

"It was about the camera. I was taking everyone's photo. My whole family—Mum, Dad, and Terry. They were barbecuing. In the back garden. I held up the camera. I kept saying, 'Say Cheese, Say Cheese', over and over again. And when I looked through the viewfinder, they were smiling back at me—but . . . they were skeletons. All of them. Their skin had gone, and—and . . ."

Greg's voice trailed off.

"What a stupid dream," Shari said, laughing.

"But that's why I don't want to bring the camera," Greg insisted. "I think—"

"Bring it, Greg," she interrupted. "It's not your camera, you know. All four of us were in the Coffman house. It belongs to all four of us. Bring it."

"But *why*, Shari?" Greg demanded.

"It'll be a laugh, that's all. It takes such weird pictures."

"That's for sure," Greg muttered.

"We don't have anything else to do for my party," Shari told him. "I wanted to rent a video, but my mum says we have to go outdoors. She doesn't want her precious house messed up. So I thought we could take everyone's picture with the weird camera. You know. See what strange things come out."

"Shari, I really don't—"

"Bring it," she ordered. And hung up.

Greg stood for a long time staring at the phone receiver, thinking hard, trying to decide what to do.

Then he replaced the receiver and headed reluctantly up to his room.

With a loud sigh, he pulled the camera from its hiding place in his headboard. "It's Shari's birthday, after all," he said aloud to himself.

His hands were trembling as he picked it

up. He realized he was afraid of it.

I shouldn't be doing this, he thought, feeling a tight knot of dread in the pit of his stomach.

I know I shouldn't be doing this.

"How's it going, Bird?" Greg called, making his way across the flagstone patio to Shari's back garden.

"I'm feeling okay," Bird said, slapping his friend a high five. "The only problem is, ever since that ball hit me," Bird continued, frowning, "from time to time I start—*pluuccck cluuuck cluuuuuuck!*—clucking like a chicken!" He flapped his arms and started strutting across the back garden, clucking at the top of his voice.

"Hey, Bird—go lay an egg!" someone yelled, and everyone laughed.

"Bird's at it again," Michael said, shaking his head. He gave Greg a friendly punch on the shoulder. Michael, his red hair unbrushed as usual, was wearing faded jeans and a flowered Hawaiian sports shirt about three sizes too big for him.

"*Where*'d you find that shirt?" Greg asked,

holding Michael at arm's length by the shoulders to admire it.

"In a cereal box," Bird chimed in, still flapping his arms.

"My grandmother gave it to me," Michael said, frowning.

"He made it in home economics," Bird interrupted. One joke was never enough.

"But why did you *wear* it?" Greg asked.

Michael shrugged. "Everything else was dirty."

Bird bent down, picked up a small clump of soil from the lawn, and rubbed it on the back of Michael's shirt. "Now this one's dirty, too," he declared.

"Hey, you—" Michael reacted with playful anger, grabbing Bird and shoving him into the hedge.

"Did you bring it?"

Hearing Shari's voice, Greg turned towards the house and saw her jogging across the patio in his direction. Her black hair was pulled back in a single plait, and she had on an oversized, silky yellow top that came down over black lycra leggings.

"Did you bring it?" she repeated eagerly. A charm bracelet filled with tiny silver charms—a birthday present—jangled at her wrist.

"Yeah." Greg reluctantly held up the camera.

"Excellent," she declared.

"I really don't want—" Greg started.

"You can take *my* picture first seeing as it's my birthday," Shari interrupted. "Here. How's this?" She struck a sophisticated pose, leaning against a tree with her hand behind her head.

Greg obediently raised the camera. "Are you sure you want me to do this, Shari?"

"Yeah. Come on. I want to take everyone's picture."

"But it'll probably come out weird," Greg protested.

"I know," Shari replied impatiently, holding her pose. "That's the fun of it."

"But, Shari—"

"Michael puked on his shirt," he heard Bird telling someone near the hedge.

"I did not!" Michael was screaming.

"You mean it looks like that *naturally*?" Bird asked.

Greg could hear a lot of raucous laughing, all of it at Michael's expense.

"Will you take the picture!" Shari cried, holding on to the slender trunk of the tree.

Greg pointed the lens at her and pressed the button. The camera whirred, and then the undeveloped, white square rolled out.

"Hey, are we the only boys invited?" Michael asked, walking up to Shari.

"Yeah. Just you three," Shari said. "And nine girls."

"Oh, wow." Michael made a face.

"Take Michael's photo next," Shari told Greg.

"No way!" Michael replied quickly, raising his hands as if to shield himself and backing away. "The last time you took my photograph with that thing, I fell down the stairs."

Trying to get away, Michael backed right into Nina Blake, one of Shari's friends. She reacted with a squeal of surprise, then gave him a playful shove, and he kept right on backing away.

"Michael, come on. It's *my* party," Shari called.

"What are we going to do? Is this *it*?" Nina demanded from halfway across the garden.

"I thought we'd take everyone's photo and then play a game or something," Shari told her.

"A game?" Bird chimed in. "You mean like Spin the Bottle?"

A few kids laughed.

"Truth or Dare!" Nina suggested.

"Yeah. Truth or Dare!" a couple of other girls called in agreement.

"Oh, no," Greg groaned quietly to himself. Truth or Dare meant a lot of kissing and awkward, embarrassing stunts.

Nine girls and only three boys.

It was going to be *really* embarrassing.

How could Shari *do* this to us? he wondered.

"Well, did it come out?" Shari asked, grabbing

his arm. "Let me see."

Greg was so upset about having to play Truth or Dare, he had forgotten about the photo developing in his hand. He held it up, and they both examined it.

"Where am I?" Shari asked in surprise. "What were you aiming at? You missed me!"

"Huh?" Greg stared at the snapshot. There was the tree. But no Shari. "Weird! I pointed it straight at you. I lined it up carefully," he protested.

"Well, you missed me. I'm not in the photo," Shari replied disgustedly.

"But, Shari—"

"I mean, come *on*—I'm not invisible, Greg. I'm not a vampire or something. I can see my reflection in mirrors. And I do usually show up in photos."

"But, look—" Greg stared hard at the photograph. "There's the tree you were leaning against. You can see the trunk clearly. And there's the spot where you were standing."

"But where *am* I?" Shari demanded, jangling her charm bracelet noisily. "Never mind." She grabbed the picture from him and tossed it on the grass. "Take another one. Quick."

"Well, okay. But—" Greg was still puzzling over the photo. Why hadn't Shari shown up in it? He bent down, picked it up, and shoved it into his pocket.

"Stand closer this time," she instructed.

Greg moved a few steps closer, carefully centred Shari in the viewfinder, and snapped the picture. A square of film zipped out of the front.

Shari walked over and pulled the picture from the camera. "This one had better come out," she said, staring hard at it as the colours began to darken and take form.

"If you really want pictures of everyone, we should get another camera," Greg said, his eyes also locked on the snapshot.

"Hey—I don't *believe* it!" Shari cried.

Again, she was invisible.

The tree photographed clearly, in perfect focus. But Shari was nowhere to be seen.

"You were right. The stupid camera is broken," she said disgustedly, handing the photo to Greg. "Forget it." She turned away from him and called to the others. "Hey, boys—Truth or Dare!"

There were some cheers and some groans.

Shari headed them back to the woods behind her back garden to play. "More privacy," she explained. There was a circular clearing just beyond the trees, a perfect, private place.

The game was just as embarrassing as Greg had imagined. Among the boys, only Bird seemed to be enjoying it. Bird loves stupid stuff like this, Greg thought, with some envy.

Luckily, after little more than half an hour, he

heard Mrs Walker, Shari's mum, calling from the house, summoning them back to cut the birthday cake.

"Aw, too bad," Greg said sarcastically. "Just when the game was getting good."

"We have to get out of the woods, anyway," Bird said, grinning. "Michael's shirt is scaring the squirrels."

Laughing and talking about the game, the kids made their way back to the patio where the pink-and-white birthday cake, candles all lit, was waiting on the round patio table.

"I must be a pretty bad mother," Mrs Walker joked, "allowing you all to go off into the woods by yourselves."

Some of the girls laughed.

Cake knife in her hand, Mrs Walker looked around. "Where's Shari?"

Everyone turned their eyes to search the back garden. "She was with us in the woods," Nina told Mrs Walker. "Just a minute ago."

"Hey, Shari!" Bird called, cupping his hands to his mouth as a megaphone. "Earth calling Shari! It's cake time!"

No reply.

No sign of her.

"Did she go into the house?" Greg asked.

Mrs Walker shook her head. "No. She didn't come past the patio. Is she still in the woods?"

"I'll go and check," Bird told her. Calling

Shari's name, he ran to the edge of the trees at the back of the garden. Then he disappeared into the trees, still calling.

A few minutes later, Bird emerged, signalling to the others with a shrug.

No sign of her.

They searched the house. The front garden. The woods again.

But Shari had vanished.

Greg sat in the shade with his back against the tree trunk, the camera on the ground at his side, and watched the blue-uniformed policemen.

They covered the back garden and could be seen bending low as they climbed around in the woods. He could hear their voices, but couldn't make out what they were saying. Their faces were intent, bewildered.

More policemen arrived, grim-faced, business-like.

And then, even more dark-uniformed police-men.

Mrs Walker had called her husband home from a golf game. They sat huddled together on canvas chairs in a corner of the patio. They whispered to each other, their eyes darting across the garden. Holding hands, they looked pale and worried.

Everyone else had left.

On the patio, the table was still set. The

birthday candles had burned all the way down, the blue and red wax melting in hard puddles on the pink-and-white icing, the cake untouched.

"No sign of her," a red-cheeked policeman with a white-blond moustache was telling the Walkers. He pulled off his cap and scratched his head, revealing short, blond hair.

"Did someone . . . take her away?" Mr Walker asked, still holding his wife's hand.

"No sign of a struggle," the policeman said. "No sign of anything, really."

Mrs Walker sighed loudly and lowered her head. "I just don't understand it."

There was a long, painful silence.

"We'll keep looking," the policeman said. "I'm sure we'll find . . . something."

He turned and headed towards the woods.

"Oh. Hi." He stopped in front of Greg, staring down at him as if seeing him for the first time. "You still here, son? All the other guests have gone home." He pushed his hair back and replaced his cap.

"Yeah, I know," Greg replied solemnly, lifting the camera into his lap.

"I'm Officer Riddick," he said.

"Yeah, I know," Greg repeated softly.

"How come you didn't go home after we'd talked with you, like the others?" Riddick asked.

"I'm just upset, I suppose," Greg told him. "I mean, Shari's a good friend, you know?" He cleared his throat, which felt dry and tight. "Besides, I live just over there." He gestured with his head to his house next door.

"Well, you might as well go home, son," Riddick said, turning his eyes to the woods with a frown. "This search could take a long time. We haven't found a thing back there yet."

"I know," Greg replied, rubbing his hand against the back of the camera.

And I know that this camera is the reason Shari is missing, he thought, feeling miserable and frightened.

"One minute she was there. The next minute she had gone," the policeman said, studying Greg's face as if looking for answers there.

"Yeah," Greg replied. "It's so weird."

It's weirder than anyone knows, he thought.

The camera made her invisible. The camera did it.

First, she vanished from the photo.

Then she vanished in real life.

The camera did it to her. I don't know how. But it did.

"Do you have something more to tell me?" Riddick asked, hands resting on his hips, his right hand just above the worn brown holster that carried his pistol. "Did you see something? Something that might give us a clue, help us out? Something you didn't remember to tell me before?"

Should I tell him? Greg wondered.

If I tell him about the camera, he'll ask where I got it. And I'll have to tell him that I got it in the Coffman house. And we'll get into trouble for breaking in there.

But—big deal. Shari is missing. Gone. Vanished. That's a lot more important.

I should tell him, Greg decided.

But then he hesitated. If I tell him, he won't believe me.

If I tell him, how will it help bring Shari back?

"You look very troubled," Riddick said, squatting down next to Greg in the shade. "What's your name again?"

"Greg. Greg Banks."

"Well, you look very troubled, Greg," the policeman repeated softly. "Why don't you tell me what's bothering you? Why don't you tell me what's on your mind? I think it'll make you feel a lot better."

Greg took a deep breath and glanced up to the patio. Mrs Walker had covered her face with her hands. Her husband was leaning over her, trying to comfort her.

"Well . . ." Greg started.

"Go ahead, son," Riddick urged softly. "Do you know where Shari is?"

"It's the camera," Greg blurted out. He could suddenly feel the blood throbbing against his temples.

He took a deep breath and then continued. "You see, this camera is weird."

"What do you mean?" Riddick asked quietly.

Greg took another deep breath. "I took Shari's photograph. Before. When I first arrived. I took two photos. And she was invisible. In both of them. See?"

Riddick closed his eyes, then opened them. "No. I don't understand."

"Shari was invisible in the photo. Everything else was there. But she wasn't. She had vanished, see. And, then, later, she vanished for real. The camera—it predicts the future, I think. Or it makes bad things happen." Greg raised the camera, attempting to hand it to the policeman.

Riddick made no attempt to take it. He just stared hard at Greg, his eyes narrowing, his expression hardening.

Greg felt a sudden stab of fear.

Oh, no, he thought. Why is he looking at me like that?

What is he going to do?

Greg continued to hold the camera out to the policeman.

But Riddick quickly climbed to his feet. "The camera makes bad things happen?" His eyes burned into Greg's.

"Yes," Greg told him. "It isn't my camera, see? And every time I take a photo—"

"Son, that's enough," Riddick said gently. He reached down and rested a hand on Greg's trembling shoulder. "I think you're very upset, Greg," he said, his voice almost a whisper. "I don't blame you. This is very upsetting for everyone."

"But it's *true*—" Greg began to insist.

"I'm going to ask that officer over there," Riddick said, pointing, "to take you home now. And I'm going to ask him to tell your parents that you've been through a very frightening experience."

I *knew* he wouldn't believe me, Greg thought angrily.

How could I have been so stupid?

Now he thinks I'm some kind of a nut case.

Riddick called to a policeman at the side of the house near the hedge.

"No, that's okay," Greg said, quickly pulling himself up, cradling the camera in his hand. "I can make it home okay."

Riddick eyed him suspiciously. "You sure?"

"Yeah. I can walk by myself."

"If you have anything to tell me later," Riddick said, lowering his gaze to the camera, "just call the station, okay?"

"Okay," Greg replied, walking slowly towards the front of the house.

"Don't worry, Greg. We'll do our best," Riddick called after him. "We'll find her. Put the camera away and try to get some rest, okay?"

"Okay," Greg muttered.

He hurried past the Walkers, who were still huddled together under the parasol on the patio.

Why was I so stupid? he asked himself as he walked home. Why did I expect that policeman to believe such a weird story?

I'm not even sure I believe it myself.

A few minutes later, he pulled open the back door and entered his kitchen. "Anybody home?"

No reply.

He headed through the back hall towards the living room. "Anyone home?"

No one.

Terry was at work. His mother must be visiting his dad at the hospital.

Greg felt depressed. He really didn't feel like being alone now. He really wanted to tell them about what had happened to Shari. He really wanted to talk to them.

Still cradling the camera, he climbed the stairs to his room.

He stopped in the doorway, blinked twice, then uttered a cry of horror.

His books were scattered all over the floor. The covers had been pulled off his bed. His desk drawers were all open, their contents strewn around the room. The desk lamp was on its side on the floor. All of his clothes had been pulled from the chest of drawers and his wardrobe and tossed everywhere.

Someone had been in Greg's room—and had turned it upside down!

Who would do this? Greg asked himself, staring in horror at his ransacked room.

Who would tear my room apart like this?

He realized that he knew the answer. He knew who would do it, who *had* done it.

Someone looking for the camera.

Someone desperate to get the camera back.

Spidey?

The creepy man who dressed all in black was living in the Coffman house. Was he the owner of the camera?

Yes, Greg knew, Spidey had done it.

Spidey had been watching Greg, spying on Greg from behind the benches at the Little League game.

He knew that Greg had his camera. *And he knew where Greg lived.*

That thought was the most chilling of all.

He knew where Greg lived.

Greg turned away from the chaos in his room,

leaned against the wall of the hallway, and closed his eyes.

He pictured Spidey, the dark figure creeping along so evilly on his spindly legs. He pictured him inside the house, Greg's house. Inside Greg's room.

He was here, thought Greg. He pawed through all my things. He wrecked my room.

Greg stepped back into his room. He felt all mixed up. He felt like shouting angrily and crying for help all at once.

But he was all alone. No one to hear him. No one to help him.

What now? he wondered. What now?

Suddenly, leaning against the doorframe, staring at his ransacked room, he knew what he had to do.

"Hey, Bird, it's me."

Greg held the receiver in one hand and wiped the sweat off his forehead with the other. He'd never worked so hard—or so fast—in all his life.

"Did they find Shari?" Bird asked eagerly.

"I haven't heard. I don't think so," Greg said, his eyes surveying his room. Almost back to normal.

He had put everything back, cleaned and straightened. His parents would never guess.

"Listen, Bird, I'm not calling about that," Greg said, speaking rapidly into the phone. "Phone Michael for me, okay? Meet me at the playground. By the baseball pitch."

"When? Now?" Bird asked, sounding confused.

"Yeah," Greg told him. "We have to meet. It's important."

"It's almost dinnertime," Bird protested. "I don't know if my parents—"

"It's important," Greg repeated impatiently. "I've got to see you both. Okay?"

"Well . . . maybe I can sneak out for a few minutes," Bird said, lowering his voice. And then Greg heard him shout to his mother. "It's no one, Ma! I'm talking to no one!"

Boy, *that's* quick thinking! Greg thought sarcastically. He's a worse liar than I am!

And then he heard Bird call to his mum! "I *know* I'm on the phone. But I'm not talking to anyone. It's only Greg."

Thanks a lot, pal, Greg thought.

"I gotta go," Bird said.

"Get Michael, okay?" Greg urged.

"Yeah. Okay. See you." He hung up.

Greg replaced the receiver, then listened for his mother. Silence downstairs. She still wasn't home. She didn't know about Shari, Greg realized. He knew she and his dad were going to be very upset.

Very upset.

Almost as upset as he was.

Thinking about his missing friend, he went to his bedroom window and looked down on her garden next door. It was deserted now.

The policemen had all left. Shari's shaken parents must have gone inside.

A squirrel sat under the wide shade of the big tree, gnawing furiously at an acorn, another acorn at his feet.

91

In the corner of the window, Greg could see the birthday cake, still sitting forlornly on the deserted table, the places all set, the decorations still standing.

A birthday party for ghosts.

Greg shuddered.

"Shari is alive," he said aloud. "They'll find her. She's alive."

He knew what he had to do now.

Forcing himself away from the window, he hurried to meet his two friends.

"No way," Bird said heatedly, leaning against the bench. "Have you gone totally bananas?"

Swinging the camera by its cord, Greg turned hopefully to Michael. But Michael avoided Greg's stare. "I'm with Bird," he said, his eyes on the camera.

Since it was just about dinnertime, the playground was nearly deserted. A few little kids were on the swings at the other end. Two kids were riding their bikes round and round the playing field.

"I thought maybe you two would come with me," Greg said, disappointed. He kicked up a clump of grass with his trainer. "I have to return this thing," he continued, raising the camera. "I know it's what I have to do. I have to put it back where I found it."

"No way," Bird repeated, shaking his head. "I'm not going back to the Coffman house. Once was enough."

"Chicken?" Greg asked angrily.

"Yeah," Bird quickly admitted.

"You don't have to take it back," Michael argued. He pulled himself up the side of the benches, climbed onto the third deck of seats, then lowered himself to the ground.

"What do you mean?" Greg asked impatiently, kicking at the grass.

"Just dump it, Greg," Michael urged, making a throwing motion with one hand. "Chuck it. Throw it away somewhere."

"Yeah. Or leave it right here," Bird suggested. He reached for the camera. "Give it to me. I'll hide it under the seats."

"You don't understand," Greg said, swinging the camera out of Bird's reach. "Throwing it away won't do any good."

"Why not?" Bird asked, making another swipe for the camera.

"Spidey'll just come back for it," Greg told him heatedly. "He'll come back to my room looking for it. He'll come after me. I know it."

"But what if we get caught taking it back?" Michael asked.

"Yeah. What if Spidey's there in the Coffman house, and he catches us?" Bird said.

"You don't understand," Greg cried. "He knows where I live! He was in my house. He was in my *room*! He wants his camera back, and—"

"Here. Give it to me," Bird said. "We don't have to go back to that house. He can find it. Right here."

He grabbed again for the camera.

Greg held tightly to the strap and tried to tug it away.

But Bird grabbed the side of the camera.

"No!" Greg cried out as it flashed. And whirred.

A square of film slid out.

"No!" Greg cried to Bird, horrified, staring at the white square as it started to develop. "You took *my* picture!"

His hand trembling, he pulled the photo from the camera.

What would it show?

95

"Sorry," Bird said. "I didn't mean to—"

Before he could finish his sentence, a voice interrupted from behind the benches. "Hey— what've you got there?"

Greg looked up from the developing photograph in surprise. Two tough-looking boys stepped out of the shadows, their expressions hard, their eyes on the camera.

He recognized them immediately—Joey Ferris and Mickey Ward—two ninth-graders who hung around together, always swaggering around, acting tough, picking on kids younger than them.

Their speciality was taking kids' bikes, riding off on them, and dumping them somewhere. There was a rumour going around school that Mickey had once beaten up a kid so badly that the kid was crippled for life. But Greg believed Mickey had made up that rumour and spread it himself.

Both boys were big for their age. Neither of them did very well at school. And even though they were always stealing bikes and skateboards, and terrorizing little kids, and getting into fights, neither of them ever seemed to get into serious trouble.

Joey had short blond hair, slicked straight up, and wore a diamond-like stud in one ear. Mickey had a round, red face full of pimples, stringy black hair down to his shoulders, and was working a toothpick between his teeth. Both boys were wearing heavy T-shirts and jeans.

"Hey, I've gotta get home," Bird said quickly, half-stepping, half-dancing away from the benches.

"Me, too," Michael said, unable to keep the fear from showing on his face.

Greg tucked the photo into his jeans pocket.

"Hey, you found my camera," Joey said, grabbing it out of Greg's hand. His small, grey eyes burned into Greg's as if searching for a reaction. "Thanks, man."

"Give it back, Joey," Greg said with a sigh.

"Yeah. Don't take that camera," Mickey told his friend, a smile spreading over his round face. "It's *mine*!" He wrestled the camera away from Joey.

"Give it back," Greg insisted angrily, reaching out his hand. Then he softened his tone. "Come on. It isn't mine."

"I *know* it isn't yours," Mickey said, grinning. "Because it's *mine!*"

"I have to give it back to the owner," Greg told him, trying not to whine, but hearing his voice edge up.

"No, you don't. I'm the owner now," Mickey insisted.

"Haven't you ever heard of finders keepers?" Joey asked, leaning over Greg menacingly. He was about six inches taller than Greg, and a lot more muscular.

"Hey, let him have the thing," Michael whispered in Greg's ear. "You wanted to get rid of it—right?"

"No!" Greg protested.

"What's your problem, Freckle Face?" Joey asked Michael, eyeing Michael up and down.

"No problem," Michael said meekly.

"Hey—say cheese!" Mickey aimed the camera at Joey.

"Don't do it," Bird interrupted, waving his hands frantically.

"Why not?" Joey demanded.

"Because your face will break the camera," Bird said, laughing.

"You're really funny," Joey said sarcastically, narrowing his eyes threateningly, hardening his features. "You want that stupid smile to be permanent?" He raised a big fist.

"I know this kid," Mickey told Joey, pointing

at Bird. "Thinks he's hot stuff."

Both boys stared hard at Bird, trying to scare him.

Bird swallowed hard. He took a step back, bumping into the benches. "No, I don't," he said softly. "I don't think I'm hot stuff."

"He looks like something I stepped in yesterday," Joey said.

He and Mickey cracked up, laughing high-pitched hyena laughs and slapping each other high fives.

"Listen, you two. I really need the camera back," Greg said, reaching out a hand to take it. "It isn't any good, anyway. It's broken. And it doesn't belong to me."

"Yeah, that's right. It's broken," Michael added, nodding his head.

"Yeah. Right," Mickey said sarcastically. "Let's just see." He raised the camera again and pointed it at Joey.

"Really. I need it back," Greg said desperately.

If they took a picture with the camera, Greg realized, they might discover its secret. That its pictures showed the future, showed only bad things happening to people. That the camera was evil. Maybe it even *caused* evil.

"Say cheese," Mickey instructed Joey.

"Just snap the stupid thing!" Joey replied impatiently.

No, Greg thought. I can't let this happen. I've got to return the camera to the Coffman house, to Spidey.

Impulsively, Greg leapt forward. With a cry, he snatched the camera away from Mickey's face.

"Hey—" Mickey reacted in surprise.

"Let's *go!*" Greg shouted to Bird and Michael.

And without another word, the three friends turned and began running across the deserted playground towards their homes.

His heart thudding in his chest, Greg gripped the camera tightly and ran as fast as he could, his trainers pounding over the dry grass.

They're going to catch us, Greg thought, panting loudly now as he raced towards the street. They're going to catch us and pound us. They're going to take back the camera. We're dead meat. Dead meat.

Greg and his friends didn't turn round until they were across the street. Breathing noisily, they looked back—and cried out in relieved surprise.

Joey and Mickey hadn't budged from beside the benches. They hadn't chased after them. They were leaning against the benches, laughing.

"Catch you later, boys!" Joey called after them.

"Yeah. Later," Mickey repeated.

They both burst out laughing again, as if they had said something hilarious.

"That was close," Michael said, still breathing hard.

"They mean it," Bird said, looking very troubled. "They'll catch us later. We're history."

"Tough talk. They're just a lot of hot air," Greg insisted.

"Oh, yeah?" Michael cried. "Then why did we run like that?"

"Because we're late for dinner," Bird joked. "See you two. I'm gonna get it if I don't hurry."

"But the camera—" Greg protested, still gripping it tightly in one hand.

"It's too late," Michael said, nervously raking a hand back through his red hair.

"Yeah. We'll have to do it tomorrow or something," Bird agreed.

"Then you'll come with me?" Greg asked eagerly.

"Uh . . . I've gotta go," Bird said without answering.

"Me, too," Michael said quickly, avoiding Greg's stare.

All three of them turned their eyes back to the playground. Joey and Mickey had disappeared. Probably off to terrorize some other kids.

"Later," Bird said, slapping Greg on the shoulder as he headed away. The three friends split up, running in different directions across lawns and drives, heading home.

Greg had run all the way to his front garden before he remembered the photograph he had shoved into his jeans pocket.

He stopped in the drive and pulled it out.

The sun was lowering behind the garage. He held the photo up close to his face to see it clearly.

"Oh, no!" he cried. "I don't believe it!"

"This is *impossible*!" Greg cried aloud, gaping at the photograph in his trembling hand.

How had Shari got into the photo?

It had been taken a few minutes before, in front of the benches on the playground.

But there was Shari, standing close beside Greg.

His hand trembling, his mouth hanging open in disbelief, Greg goggled at the photo.

It was very clear, very sharp. There they were on the playground. He could see the baseball pitch in the background.

And there they were. Greg and Shari.

Shari standing so clear, so sharp—right next to him.

And they were both staring straight ahead, their eyes wide, their mouths open, their expressions frozen in horror as a large shadow covered them both.

"Shari?" Greg cried, lowering the snapshot

and darting his eyes over the front garden. "Are you here? Can you hear me?"

He listened.

Silence.

He tried again.

"Shari? Are you here?"

"Greg!" a voice called.

Uttering a startled cry, Greg spun around. "Huh?"

"Greg!" the voice repeated. It took him a while to realize that it was his mother, calling to him from the front door.

"Oh. Hi, Mum." Feeling dazed, he slid the photo back into his jeans pocket.

"Where've you been?" his mother asked as he made his way to the door. "I heard about Shari. I've been so upset. I didn't know where you were."

"Sorry, Mum," Greg said, kissing her on the cheek. "I—I should've left a note."

He stepped into the house, feeling strange and out-of-sorts, sad and confused and frightened, all at the same time.

Two days later, on a day of high, grey clouds, the air hot and smoggy, Greg paced back and forth in his room after school.

The house was empty except for him. Terry had gone off a few hours before to his after-school job at the Dairy Freeze. Mrs Banks had driven to the hospital to pick up Greg's dad, who was finally coming home.

Greg knew he should be happy about his dad's return. But there were still too many things troubling him, tugging at his mind.

Frightening him.

For one thing, Shari still hadn't been found.

The police were completely baffled. Their new theory was that she'd been kidnapped.

Her frantic, grieving parents waited at home by the phone. But no kidnappers phoned to demand a ransom.

There were no clues of any kind.

Nothing to do but wait. And hope.

As the days passed, Greg felt more and more guilty. He was sure Shari hadn't been kidnapped. He knew that somehow, the camera had made her disappear.

But he couldn't tell anyone else what he believed.

No one would believe him. Anyone he tried to tell the story to would think he was crazy.

Cameras can't be evil, after all.

Cameras can't make people fall down stairs. Or crash their cars.

Or vanish from sight.

Cameras can only record what they see.

Greg stared out of his window, pressing his forehead against the glass, looking down on Shari's back garden. "Shari—where *are* you?"

he asked aloud, staring at the tree where she had posed.

The camera was still hidden in the secret compartment in his headboard. Neither Bird nor Michael would agree to help Greg return it to the Coffman house.

Besides, Greg had decided to hold on to it a while longer, in case he needed it as proof.

In case he decided to confide his fears about it to someone.

In case . . .

His other fear was that Spidey would come back, back to Greg's room, back for the camera.

So much to be frightened about.

He pushed himself away from the window. He had spent so much time in the past couple of days staring down at Shari's empty back garden.

Thinking. Thinking.

With a sigh, he reached into the headboard and pulled out two of the pictures he had hidden in there along with the camera.

The two photos were the ones taken the past Saturday at Shari's party. Holding one in each hand, Greg stared at them, hoping he could see something new, something he hadn't noticed before.

But the photos hadn't changed. They still showed her tree, her back garden, green in the sunlight. And no Shari. No one where Shari had been standing. As if the lens had penetrated right through her.

Staring at the photos, Greg let out a cry of anguish.

If only he had never gone into the Coffman house.

If only he had never stolen the camera.

If only he had never taken any photos with it.

If only . . . if only . . . if only . . .

Before he realized what he was doing, he was ripping the two photos into tiny pieces.

Panting loudly, his chest heaving, he tore at the pictures and let the pieces fall to the floor.

When he had ripped them both into tiny shreds of paper, he flung himself facedown on his bed and closed his eyes, waiting for his heart to stop pounding, waiting for the heavy feeling of guilt and horror to lift.

Two hours later, the phone by his bed rang.

It was Shari.

"Shari—is it really you?" Greg shouted into the phone.

"Yeah. It's me!" She sounded as surprised as he did.

"But how? I mean—" His mind was racing. He didn't know what to say.

"Your guess is as good as mine," Shari told him. And then she said, "Hold on a minute." And he heard her step away from the phone to talk to her mother. "Mum—stop crying, okay. Mum—it's really me. I'm home."

A few seconds later, she came back on the line. "I've been home for two hours, and Mum's still crying and carrying on."

"I feel like crying, too," Greg admitted. "I—I just can't believe it! Shari, where *were* you?"

The line was silent for a long moment. "I don't know," she answered finally.

"Huh?"

"I really don't. It was just so weird, Greg. One

minute, there I was at my birthday party. The next minute, I was standing in front of my house. And it was two days later. But I don't remember being away. Or being anywhere else. I don't remember anything at all."

"You don't remember going away? Or coming back?" Greg asked.

"No. Nothing," Shari said, her voice trembling.

"Shari, those pictures I took of you— remember? With the weird camera? You were invisible in them—"

"And then I disappeared," she said, finishing his thought.

"Shari, do you think—?"

"I don't know," she replied quickly. "I—I have to get off the phone now. The police are here. They want to question me. What am I going to tell them? They're going to think I had amnesia or blacked out or something."

"I—I don't know," Greg said, completely bewildered. "We have to talk. The camera—"

"I can't now," she told him. "Maybe tomorrow. Okay?" She called to her mother that she was coming. "Bye, Greg. See you." And then she hung up.

Greg replaced the receiver, but sat on the edge of his bed staring at the phone for a long time.

Shari was back.

She'd been back for about two hours.

Two hours. Two hours. Two hours.

He turned his eyes to the clock radio beside the phone.

Just two hours before, he had ripped up the two photos of an invisible Shari.

His mind whirred with wild ideas, insane ideas.

Had he brought Shari back by ripping up the photos?

Did this mean that the camera had *caused* her to disappear? That the camera had *caused* all of the terrible things that showed up in its photographs?

Greg stared at the phone for a long time, thinking hard.

He knew what he had to do. He had to talk to Shari. And he had to return the camera.

He met Shari in the playground the next afternoon. The sun floated high in a cloudless sky. Eight or nine kids were engaged in a noisy brawl of a soccer game, running one way, then the other across the outfield of the baseball diamond.

"Hey—you look like *you*!" Greg exclaimed as Shari came jogging up to where he stood beside the benches. He pinched her arm. "Yeah. It's you, okay."

She didn't smile. "I feel fine," she told him, rubbing her arm. "Just confused. And tired. The police asked me questions for hours. And when they finally went away, my parents started up."

"Sorry," Greg said quietly, staring down at his trainers.

"I think Mum and Dad believe that somehow it's my fault that I disappeared," Shari said, resting her back against the side of the benches, shaking her head.

"It's the camera's fault," Greg muttered. He raised his eyes to hers. "The camera is evil."

Shari shrugged. "Maybe. I don't know what to think. I really don't."

He showed her the photo, the one showing the two of them in the playground staring in horror as a shadow crept over them.

"How weird," Shari exclaimed, studying it hard.

"I want to take the camera back to the Coffman house," Greg said heatedly. "I can go home and get it now. Will you help me? Will you come with me?"

Shari started to reply, but stopped.

They both saw the dark shadow move, sliding towards them quickly, silently, over the grass.

And then they saw the man dressed all in black, his spindly legs pumping hard as he came at them.

Spidey!

Greg grabbed Shari's hand, frozen in fear.

He and Shari gasped in terror as Spidey's slithering shadow crept over them.

Greg had a shudder of recognition. He knew the photograph had just come true.

As the dark figure of Spidey moved towards them like a black tarantula, Greg pulled Shari's hand. "Run!" he cried in a shrill voice he didn't recognize.

He didn't have to say it. They were both running now, gasping as they ran across the grass towards the street. Their trainers thudded loudly on the ground as they reached the pavement and kept running.

Greg turned to see Spidey closing the gap. "He's catching up!" he managed to cry to Shari, who was a few steps ahead of him.

Spidey, his face still hidden in the shadows of his black baseball cap, moved with startling speed, his long legs kicking high as he pursued them.

"He's going to catch us!" Greg cried, feeling as if his chest were about to burst. "He's ... too ... fast!"

Spidey moved even closer, his shadow scuttling over the grass.

Closer.

When the car horn honked, Greg screamed.

He and Shari stopped short.

The horn blasted out again.

Greg turned to see a familiar young man inside a small hatchback. It was Jerry Norman, who lived across the street. Jerry lowered his car window. "Is this man chasing you?" he asked excitedly. Without waiting for an answer, he backed the car towards Spidey. "I'm calling the cops, mister!"

Spidey didn't reply. Instead, he turned and darted across the street.

"I'm warning you—" Jerry called after him.

But Spidey had disappeared behind a tall hedge.

"Are you kids okay?" Greg's neighbour demanded.

"Yeah. Fine," Greg managed to reply, still breathing hard, his chest heaving.

"We're okay. Thanks, Jerry," Shari said.

"I've seen that man around the neighbourhood," the young man said, staring through the windscreen at the tall hedge. "Never thought he was dangerous. You kids want me to call the police?"

"No. It's okay," Greg replied.

As soon as I give him back his camera, he'll

stop chasing us, Greg thought.

"Well, be careful—okay?" Jerry said. "You need a lift home or anything?" He studied their faces as if trying to determine how frightened and upset they were.

Greg and Shari both shook their heads. "We'll be okay," Greg said. "Thanks."

Jerry warned them once again to be careful, then drove off, his tyres squealing as he turned the corner.

"That was close," Shari said, her eyes on the hedge. "Why was Spidey chasing us?"

"He thought I had the camera. He wants it back," Greg told her. "Meet me tomorrow, okay? In front of the Coffman house. Help me put it back?"

Shari stared at him without replying, her expression thoughtful, wary.

"We're going to be in danger—all of us—until we put that camera back," Greg insisted.

"Okay," Shari said quietly. "Tomorrow."

Something scurried through the tall weeds of the unmowed front lawn. "What *was* that?" Shari cried, whispering even though no one else was in sight. "It was too big to be a squirrel."

She lingered behind Greg, who stopped to look up at the Coffman house. "Maybe it was a racoon or something," Greg told her. He gripped the camera tightly in both hands.

It was a little after three o'clock the next afternoon, a hazy, overcast day. Mountains of dark clouds threatening rain were rolling across the sky, stretching behind the house, bathing it in shadow.

"It's going to storm," Shari said, staying close behind Greg. "Let's get this over with and go home."

"Good idea," he said, glancing up at the heavy sky.

Thunder rumbled in the distance, a low roar. The old trees that dotted the front garden whispered and shook.

"We can't just run inside," Greg told her, watching the sky darken. "First we've got to make sure Spidey isn't there."

Making their way quickly through the tall grass and weeds, they stopped at the living room window and peered in. Thunder rumbled, low and long, in the distance. Greg thought he saw another creature scuttle through the weeds around the corner of the house.

"It's too dark in there. I can't see a thing," Shari complained.

"Let's check out the basement," Greg suggested. "That's where Spidey hangs out, remember?"

The sky darkened to an eerie grey-green as they made their way to the back of the house and dropped to their knees to peer down through the basement windows at ground level.

Squinting through the dust-covered windowpanes they could see the makeshift, plywood table Spidey had made, the wardrobe against the wall, its doors still open, the colourful, old clothing spilling out, the empty frozen food boxes scattered on the floor.

"No sign of him," Greg whispered, cradling the camera in his arm as if it might try to escape from him if he didn't hold it tightly. "Let's get moving."

"Are—are you sure?" Shari stammered. She

wanted to be brave. But the thought that she had disappeared for two days—completely *vanished*, most likely because of the camera—that frightening thought lingered in her mind.

Michael and Bird were chicken, she thought. But maybe they were the clever ones.

She wished this were over. All over.

A few seconds later, Greg and Shari pushed open the front door. They stepped into the darkness of the front hall. And stopped.

And listened.

And then they both jumped at the sound of the loud, sudden crash directly behind them.

Shari was the first to regain her voice. "It's just the door!" she cried. "The wind—"

A gust of wind had made the front door slam.

"Let's get this over with," Greg whispered, badly shaken.

"We never should've broken into this house in the first place," Shari whispered as they made their way on tiptoe, step by creaking step, down the dark hallway towards the basement stairs.

"It's a little late for that," Greg replied sharply.

Pulling open the door to the basement steps, he stopped again. "What's that banging sound upstairs?"

Shari's features tightened in fear as she heard it too, a repeated, almost rhythmic banging.

"Shutters?" Greg suggested.

"Yeah," she agreed quickly, breathing a sigh of relief. "A lot of the shutters are loose, remember?"

The whole house seemed to groan.

Thunder rumbled outside, closer now.

They stepped onto the landing, then waited for their eyes to adjust to the darkness.

"Couldn't we just leave the camera up here, and run?" Shari asked, more of a plea than a question.

"No. I want to put it back," Greg insisted.

"But, Greg—" She tugged at his arm as he started down the stairs.

"No!" He pulled out of her grasp. "He was in my *room*, Shari! He tore everything apart, looking for it. I want him to find it where it belongs. If he doesn't find it, he'll come back to my house. I *know* he will!"

"Okay, okay. Let's just hurry."

It was brighter in the basement, grey light seeping down from the four ground-level windows. Outside, the wind swirled and pushed against the windowpanes. A pale flash of lightning made shadows flicker against the basement wall. The old house groaned as if unhappy about the storm.

"What was *that*? Footsteps?" Shari stopped halfway across the basement and listened.

"It's just the house," Greg insisted. But his quivering voice revealed that he was as frightened as his companion, and he stopped to listen, too.

Bang. Bang. Bang.

The shutter high above them continued its rhythmic pounding.

"Where did you find the camera, anyway?" Shari whispered, following Greg to the far wall opposite the enormous boiler with its cobwebbed ducts sprouting up like pale tree limbs.

"Over here," Greg told her. He stepped up to the worktable and reached for the vice clamped on the edge. "When I turned the vice, a door opened up. Some kind of hidden shelf. That's where the camera—"

He cranked the handle of the vice.

Once again, the door to the secret shelf popped open.

"Good," he whispered excitedly. He flashed Shari a smile.

He shoved the camera onto the shelf, tucking the carrying strap under it. Then he pushed the door closed. "We're out of here."

He felt so much better. So relieved. So much *lighter*.

The house groaned and creaked. Greg didn't care.

Another flash of lightning, brighter this time, like a camera flash, sent shadows flickering on the wall.

"Come on," he whispered. But Shari was already ahead of him, making her way carefully over the empty food cartons strewn everywhere, hurrying towards the steps.

They were halfway up the stairs, Greg one step behind Shari, when, above them, Spidey stepped silently into view on the landing, blocking their escape.

29

Greg blinked and shook his head, as if he could shake away the image of the figure that stared darkly down at him.

"No!" Shari cried out, and fell back against Greg.

He grabbed for the railing, forgetting that it had fallen under Michael's weight during their first unfortunate visit to the house. Luckily, Shari regained her balance before toppling them both down the stairs.

Lightning flashed behind them, sending a flash of white light across the staircase. But the unmoving figure on the landing above them remained shrouded in darkness.

"Let us go!" Greg finally managed to cry, finding his voice.

"Yeah. We've brought back your camera!" Shari added, sounding shrill and frightened.

Spidey didn't reply. Instead, he took a step towards them, onto the first step. And then he descended another step.

Nearly stumbling again, Greg and Shari backed down to the basement floor.

The wooden stairs squeaked in protest as the dark figure stepped slowly, steadily, down. As he reached the basement floor, a crackling bolt of lightning cast a blue light over him, and Greg and Shari saw his face for the first time.

In the brief flash of colour, they saw that he was old, older than they had imagined. That his eyes were small and round like dark marbles. That his mouth was small, too, pursed in a tight, menacing grimace.

"We returned the camera," Shari said, staring in fear as Spidey crept closer. "Can't we go now? Please?"

"Let me see," Spidey said. His voice was younger than his face, warmer than his eyes. "Come."

They hesitated. But he gave them no choice.

Ushering them back across the cluttered floor to the worktable, he wrapped his large, spidery hand over the vice and turned the handle. The door opened. He pulled out the camera and held it close to his face to examine it.

"You shouldn't have taken it," he told them, speaking softly, turning the camera in his hands.

"We're sorry," Shari said quickly.

"Can we go now?" Greg asked, edging towards the stairs.

"It's not an ordinary camera," Spidey said, raising his small eyes to them.

"We know," Greg blurted out. "The pictures it took. They—"

Spidey's eyes grew wide, his expression angry. "You took pictures with it?"

"Just a few," Greg told him, wishing he had kept his mouth shut. "They didn't come out. Really."

"You know about the camera, then," Spidey said, moving quickly to the middle of the floor.

Was he trying to block their escape? Greg wondered.

"It's broken or something," Greg said uncertainly, shoving his hands into his jeans pockets.

"It's not broken," the tall, dark figure said softly. "It's evil." He motioned towards the low plywood table. "Sit there."

Shari and Greg exchanged glances. Then, reluctantly, they sat down on the edge of the board, sitting stiffly, nervously, their eyes darting towards the staircase, towards escape.

"The camera is evil," Spidey repeated, standing over them, holding the camera in both hands. "I should know. I helped to create it."

"You're an inventor?" Greg asked, glancing at Shari, who was nervously tugging at a strand of her black hair.

"I'm a scientist," Spidey replied. "Or, I should

125

say, I *was* a scientist. My name is Fredericks. Dr Fritz Fredericks." He transferred the camera from one hand to the other. "My lab partner invented this camera. It was his pride and joy. More than that, it would have made him a fortune. *Would* have, I say." He paused, a thoughtful expression sinking over his face.

"What happened to him? Did he die?" Shari asked, still fiddling with the strand of hair.

Dr Fredricks sniggered. "No. Worse. I stole the invention from him. I stole the plans and the camera. I was evil, you see. I was young and greedy. So very greedy. And I wasn't above stealing to make my fortune."

He paused, eyeing them both as if waiting for them to say something, to offer their disapproval of him, perhaps. But when Greg and Shari remained silent, staring up at him from the low plywood table, he continued his story.

"When I stole the camera, it caught my partner by surprise. Unfortunately, from then on, all of the surprises were mine." A strange, sad smile twisted across his aged face. "My partner, you see, was much more evil than I was."

Dr Fredericks coughed into his hand, then began to pace in front of Greg and Shari as he talked, speaking softly, slowly, as if remembering the story for the first time in a long while.

"My partner was a *true* evil one. He dabbled in

126

black magic. I should correct myself. He didn't just dabble. He was quite a master of it all."

He held up the camera, waving it above his head, then lowering it. "My partner put a curse on the camera. If he couldn't profit from it, he wanted to make sure that I never would, either. And so he put a curse on it."

He turned his gaze on Greg, leaning over him. "Do you know about how some primitive peoples fear the camera? They fear the camera because they believe that if it takes their picture, it will steal their soul." He patted the camera. "Well, this camera really *does* steal souls."

Staring up at the camera, Greg shuddered.

The camera had stolen Shari away.

Would it have stolen *all* of their souls?

"People have died because of this camera," Dr Fredericks said, uttering a slow, sad sigh. "People close to me. That's how I came to learn of the curse, to learn of the camera's evil. And then I learned something just as frightening— the camera cannot be destroyed."

He coughed, cleared his throat noisily, and began to pace in front of them again. "And so I vowed to keep the camera a secret. To keep it away from people so it cannot do its evil. I lost my job. My family. I lost everything because of it. But I am determined to keep the camera where it can do no harm."

He stopped pacing with his back towards them. He stood silently, shoulders hunched, lost in thought.

Greg quickly climbed to his feet and motioned for Shari to do the same. "Well...uh...I suppose it's good we returned it," he said hesitantly. "Sorry we caused so much trouble."

"Yeah, we're very sorry," Shari repeated sincerely. "It's back in the right hands now."

"Goodbye," Greg said, starting towards the steps. "It's getting late, and we—"

"No!" Dr Fredericks shouted, startling them both. He moved quickly to block the way. "I'm afraid you can't go. You know too much."

"I can never let you leave," Dr Fredericks said, his face flickering in the blue glow of a lightning flash. He crossed his bony arms in front of his black sweatshirt.

"But we won't tell anyone," Greg said, his voice rising until the words became a plea. "Really."

"Your secret is safe with us," Shari insisted, her frightened eyes on Greg.

Dr Fredericks stared at them menacingly, but didn't reply.

"You can trust us," Greg said, his voice quivering. He cast a frightened glance at Shari.

"Besides," Shari said, "even if we *did* tell anyone, who would believe us?"

"Enough talk," Dr Fredericks snapped. "It won't do you any good. I've worked too long and too hard to keep the camera a secret."

A rush of wind pushed against the windows, sending up a low howl. The wind carried a drum roll of rain. The sky through the basement windows was as black as night.

"You—can't keep us here *forever*!" Shari cried, unable to keep the growing terror from her voice.

The rain pounded against the windows now, a steady downpour.

Dr Fredericks drew himself up straight. He seemed to grow taller. His tiny eyes burned into Shari's. "I'm so sorry," he said, his voice a whisper of regret. "So sorry. But I have no choice."

He took another step towards them.

Greg and Shari exchanged frightened glances. From where they stood, in front of the low plywood table in the middle of the basement, the steps seemed a hundred miles away.

"Wh-what are you going to do?" Greg cried, shouting over a burst of thunder that rattled the basement windows.

"Please—!" Shari begged. "Don't—!"

Dr Fredericks moved forward with surprising speed. Holding the camera in one hand, he grabbed Greg's shoulder with the other.

"No!" Greg screamed. "Let go!"

"Let go of him!" Shari screamed.

She suddenly realized that both of Dr Fredericks' hands were occupied.

This may be my only chance, she thought.

She took a deep breath and lunged forward.

Dr Fredericks' eyes bulged, and he cried out in

surprise as Shari grabbed the camera with both hands and pulled it away from him. He made a frantic grab for the camera, and Greg burst free.

Before the desperate man could take another step, Shari raised the camera to her eye and pointed the lens at him.

"Please—no! Don't push the button!" the old man cried.

He lurched forward, his eyes wild, and grabbed the camera with both hands.

Greg stared in horror as Shari and Dr Fredericks grappled, both holding onto the camera, each trying desperately to wrestle it away from the other.

FLASH!

The bright burst of light startled them all.

Shari grabbed the camera. "Run!" she screamed.

The basement became a whirring blur of greys and blacks as Greg hurled himself towards the stairs.

He and Shari ran side by side, slipping over the food cartons, jumping over tin cans and empty bottles.

Rain thundered against the windows. The wind howled, pushing against the glass. They could hear Dr Fredericks' anguished screams behind them.

"Did it take our picture or his?" Shari asked.

"I don't know. Just *hurry*!" Greg screamed.

The old man was howling like a wounded animal, his cries competing with the rain and wind pushing at the windows.

The stairs weren't that far away. But it seemed to take forever to reach them.

Forever.

Forever, Greg thought. Dr Fredericks wanted to keep Shari and him down there *forever*.

Panting loudly, they both reached the dark staircase. A deafening clap of thunder made them stop and turn round.

"Huh?" Greg cried aloud.

To his shock, Dr Fredericks hadn't chased after them.

And his anguished cries had stopped.

The basement was silent.

"What's going on?" Shari cried breathlessly.

Squinting back into the darkness, it took Greg a while to realize that the dark, rumpled form lying on the floor in front of the worktable was Dr Fredericks.

"What happened?" Shari cried, her chest heaving as she struggled to catch her breath. Still clinging to the camera strap, she gaped in surprise at the old man's still body, sprawled on its back on the floor.

"I don't know," Greg replied in a breathless whisper.

Reluctantly, Greg started back towards Dr Fredericks. Following close behind, Shari uttered a low cry of horror when she clearly saw the fallen man's face.

Eyes bulged out, the mouth open in a twisted O of terror, the face stared up at them. Frozen. Dead.

Dr Fredericks was dead.

"What—*happened*?" Shari finally managed to say, swallowing hard, forcing herself to turn away from the ghastly, tortured face.

"I think he died of fright," Greg replied, squeezing her shoulder and not even realizing it.

"Huh? Fright?"

"He knew better than anyone what the camera could do," Greg said. "When you snapped his picture, I think . . . I think it scared him to *death*!"

"I only wanted to throw him off-guard," Shari cried. "I only wanted to give us a chance to escape. I didn't think—"

"The picture," Greg interrupted. "Let's see the picture."

Shari raised the camera. The photo was still half-inside the camera. Greg pulled it out with a trembling hand. He held it up so they could both see it.

"Wow," he exclaimed quietly. "Wow."

The photo showed Dr Fredericks lying on the floor, his eyes bulging, his mouth frozen open in horror.

Dr Fredericks' fright, Greg realized—the fright that had killed him—was there, frozen on film, frozen on his face.

The camera had claimed another victim. This time, forever.

"What do we do now?" Shari asked, staring down at the figure sprawled at their feet.

"First, I'm putting this camera back," Greg said, taking it from her and shoving it back on its shelf. He turned the vice handle, and the door

134

to the secret compartment closed.

Greg breathed a sigh of relief. Hiding the dreadful camera away made him feel so much better.

"Now, let's go home and call the police," he said.

Two days later, a cool, bright day with a gentle breeze rustling the trees, the four friends stopped at the kerb, leaning on their bikes, and stared up at the Coffman house. Even in bright sunlight, the old trees that surrounded the house covered it in shade.

"So you didn't tell the police about the camera?" Bird asked, staring up at the dark, empty front window.

"No. They wouldn't believe it," Greg told him. "Besides, the camera should stay locked up forever. *Forever*! I hope no one ever finds out about it."

"We told the police we ran into the house to get out of the rain," Shari added. "And we said we started to explore while we waited for the storm to blow over. And we found the body in the basement."

"What did Spidey die of?" Michael asked, gazing up at the house.

"The police said it was heart failure," Greg told him. "But we know the truth."

"Wow. I can't believe an old camera could do

so much evil," Bird said.

"I believe it," Greg said quietly.

"Let's get out of here," Michael urged. He put his trainers on the pedals and started to roll away. "This place really creeps me out."

The other three followed, pedalling away in thoughtful silence.

They had turned the corner and were heading up the next road when two figures emerged from the back door of the Coffman house. Joey Ferris and Mickey Ward stepped over the weed-choked lawn onto the drive.

"Those jerks aren't too bright," Joey told his companion. "They never even saw us the other day. Never saw us watching them through the basement window."

Mickey laughed. "Yeah. They're jerks."

"They couldn't hide this camera from *us*. No way, man," Joey said. He raised the camera and examined it.

"Take my picture," Mickey demanded. "Come on. Let's try it out."

"Yeah. Okay." Joey raised the viewfinder to his eye. "Say cheese."

A click. A flash. A whirring sound.

Joey pulled the photo from the camera, and both boys eagerly huddled around it, waiting to see what developed.

Add *more*

Goosebumps

to your collection . . .
A chilling preview of
what's next from
R.L. STINE

STAY OUT OF THE
BASEMENT

Margaret pulled the door open the rest of the way, and they stepped onto the narrow stairway. "Hey, Dad —" Casey called excitedly. "Dad — can we see?"

They were halfway down when their father appeared at the foot of the stairs. He glared up at them angrily, his skin strangely green under the fluorescent light fixture. He was holding his right hand, drops of blood falling onto his white lab coat.

"*Stay out of the basement!*" he bellowed, in a voice they'd never heard before.

Both kids shrank back, surprised to hear their father scream like that. He was usually so mild and soft-spoken.

"*Stay out of the basement,*" he repeated, holding his bleeding hand. "Don't *ever* come down here — I'm warning you."